ISBN 978-1-84481-971-X

A digital edition of this book was first published by Cool Publications in 2003

The Eclectic Book Shop Company

A catalogue record of the Book is available from the British Library

A catalogue record of this e-book is available from the British Library.

Published with the assistance of: Amerland Enterprises Ltd, 118 Gatley Road, Cheadle, Cheshire,
SK8 4AD

www.fantasynovel.co.uk

The Shade

Acknowledgements

I am, now, much wiser regarding the vagaries of publishing and the publishing process to think that talent alone can ever be the only requirement for success. In creating this book, getting it to print and then getting it to the web in this format I owe a heavy debt to more people than I can possibly cover here. Some, of course, tried to do everything else but help and to them, also, I am in debt because my inevitable interaction with them forced me to change in unanticipated ways which, ultimately, have led to my further development. I have been accused of being reclusive and this I freely admit. It is not that I do not like people, or interviews, quite on the contrary, but I dislike artifice and refuse to play games and when it comes to books really all you need to know about me and my skills are between the pages of the book you read. Anything else I add is there for public consumption and therefore suspect. So I find it easier to live away from crowds in a quiet English village at the outskirts of a major city and I read, think and write though not necessarily in that order.

Because of this my first thanks must go to David because he first saw the value in a manuscript which every other publisher had refused. And though things did not turn out all that great for him or the publishing house he worked for in the end, he never ceased to believe that what I had here was worth reading.

Thanks must also go to N. She made the technical side happen and without her I would not have bothered again, with anything.

But really, deep down, I must give thanks to Guttenberg. He stands behind the widespread practice of reading.

As an author I stand behind my creation and at its side (laugh all you can, authors can do contradictory things with ease). I owe some thanks, incredibly enough, to Jean Claude van Damm, whose bad choice in film roles and incredibly poor acting ability in one, in particular, became the seed of what is now this novel (which, I hope, will make you think twice before you argue, again, against the need for poor art).

Read it, enjoy it. If it makes you think, drop me a line at www.fantasynovel.co.uk

Tom – 2007

I dreamt a dream: I dreamt that I espied,
Upon a stone that was not rolled aside,
A Shadow sit upon a grave - a Shade,
As thin, as unsubstantial, as of old
Came, the Greek poet told,
To lick the life-blood in the trench Ulysses made-
As pale, as thin, and said:
'I am the Resurrection of the Dead.
The night is past, the morning is at hand,
And I must in my proper semblance stand...

Hugh Arnold

Chapter 1
The Nameless Town

The Slinger came out of the desert in the middle of a dream. The dream had ended and all he knew was that he was following the traitor's trail. His horse had given up its life trying to get him through the desert and he was too far gone with exhaustion to notice when the hot, shifting sand had ended and the hardened wasteland, beyond, began.

By rights he shouldn't have survived. He'd entered the desert without water. He had ignored the advice of those who'd helped him. It was a failing that had cost him a horse. He had formed a strange sort of attachment to the animal and he had been kind to it, putting it out of its misery when the moment came. This much he remembered.

Then the dream had began.

His memory focussed on the fragments he needed to complete the job at hand: He remembered that he had been kinder to the horse than he had been to the others. Those who had befriended the blond man, the traitor he was chasing. Those misguided enough to have aided him in his escape.

The Slinger's clothes, originally black, were now covered in dust. The dust had been caked into mud in places by the sweat of his body to form an encrusted armour of accumulated dirt on the fine silk fabric. Where it rubbed against the skin, the encrusted dirt and caked dust and stiffened fabric had rubbed the skin raw to form open sores.

The flesh beneath glistened red, and a clear yellowish fluid, seeped out of it.

If he felt any discomfort, the Slinger paid no attention to it. His mind was still deep in *gaffla*, the deep trance-sleep of his ancestors, whose shadows had guided him in his hour of need in the desert, when the demands of his body had at last caught up with him and death was but a step away.

There was a price to be paid for *gaffla*, he knew, but he didn't know what form it would take. The payment would not take part until he descended through the spirals, escaped the dream he could not remember and sought to inhabit the world his physical body walked in.

There was the black, leather-bound, hilt of a sword protruding over his left shoulder.

It was a long sword, in a black scabbard, slightly curved and now caked with dirt also.

The steel of the sword had been folded back one thousand times and the blade had been laboriously polished until the spirit of death it conveyed had come upon its surface and the fearful shades of steel that Slingers lived and died by shone on its edge.

There was another sword, slightly shorter, strapped to his waist. These two formed the only visible parts of his arsenal. The only statement he ever needed to make. He carried the two swords. He was a Slinger. Men gave way before him.

The spirals his spirit inhabited shortened and he sensed the physical pain begin. The agony of cells that had been left too long without water. The cries of open sores that had been rubbed raw and lost lymph fluid for too long. The ache of tired muscles that had been pushed beyond their normal limits for far too long.

Mortality.

He took a deep breath and brought the edge of his hood from around his throat to cover his mouth. He adjusted the fit round his head, leaving only his eyes exposed. The only part of his body available to the moisture-draining air surrounding him.

How had he managed to survive?

He braced himself against the rising tide of pain, squinted against the dying rays of the sun and took stock of where his steps had taken him.

It was a town. One of those that habitually sprung up at the edge of the desert to house the descendants of the round eyed strangers who mysteriously appeared from time to time and had no other place left to go.

"Kiyah!" He said to himself. His voice sounded odd to his ears. After the lengthy silence of the desert crossing it'd grown raspy and hard-edged. The vocal chords unused to speaking.

He stopped and let his eyes do the walking for him. There was a short main street, straight as an arrow, and twenty or thirty wooden buildings, closely clustered together.

When faced with the open wilderness of the wasted plain and the encroaching threat of the sand, these people, both Ronin and round-eyes, had huddled together, clustered unnecessarily close as if such proximity could drive the twin ghosts of uncertainty and danger away.

Their box-like dwellings formed two disorderly rows lining the main street, barely a spear's throw apart. Narrow claustrophobic walkways ran behind and in between them.

There was dry, throat-lining dust everywhere and not a single cobble in sight. The street was lined with rubbish, discarded pieces of used-up twine and old saddle-bags beyond any repair, and there was the feint stench of human excrement emanating from the walkways between the ramshackle houses.

He saw the faded Inn sign above the building in the centre of the town and made straight for it. At each step he was aware of eyes looking at him from behind drawn, half-broken shutters, and he gritted his teeth against the waves of pain that threatened to overcome him and kept his step steady. He was descending the spirals fast now and the pain was almost unbearable.

His memory was almost totally lost, locked within the dream he could not remember. But he had enough presence left to know that he must survive.

His first need was water.

The Inn, when he entered it, was dark.

There were several round tables inside, each with four chairs. The town's menfolk were sitting around them, drinking sake or lukewarm corn-beer and playing a game of Go. Naked torches at each corner threw a dancing, yellow light that made the shadows beneath the men's eyes appear dark, like dried up blood and the dangerous hunger on their faces, more naked.

The Slinger took all this in at a glance, saw the way the men appraised him, and turned to the lone woman behind the bar.

She was Ronin. One of the outcasts. There were long, earrings with markings worn on each ear. The markings declared her status: Courtesan.

"I want some water," the Slinger said and there was an expectant heavy silence after his words. Every eye in the Inn was upon him, silently taking in the state of his clothes and the two swords he carried.

The woman brought out a tall, long-stemmed glass and a jug of water. She put both on the bar-top, within easy reach and waited patiently.

Moving slowly, the Slinger took off his hood, shook free his long dark hair. The woman's eyes widened when she saw his features clearly but he chose to ignore it. His hand reached into one of his pockets and there was the jingle of coins, and he put one on the bar-top. It was silver, stamped with the emperor's dragon, surrounded by the thirteen Slinger stars. One for each clan.

"I have no change for it," the woman said and her eyes alternated speculatively from the coin on the bar-top to the Slinger's face.

The Slinger could see the length of faded scars disappear down the side of the woman's low-cut dress, twist away over the shoulder.

"Keep it," he said and poured the water into his glass. He had to restrain himself not to gulp it all down. Even his system would not take kindly to the shock.

There was the scraping of a chair behind him as he slowly brought the glass to his lips and he felt more than saw the studied threat of a man getting up.

The Slinger didn't turn around. He finished the motion, touched the glass to his lips and said: "Don't."

The standing man suddenly hesitated.

The man was tall, a full head taller than the Slinger, and heavyset with eyes whose epicanthic folds spoke of daily battles with the will of the desert. His hand hovered at his waist where the bony handle of a broad-bladed hunting knife protruded.

For a few long seconds nothing happened then, the standing man's companion, sitting at his table almost imperceptibly shook his head and there was an easing of the tension in the air.

The tall man sat down and looked at the top of the table in front of him. His eyes fixed on the deeply scarred surface. His features knotted.

The Slinger emptied his glass, filled it again and drunk. He repeated this until the jug was empty of water, and then looked around.

He had passed the first test.

The pain, the physical ache of thirst was slowly receding, other needs started surfacing now and he breathed a little more easily. He was fully back in the world his body inhabited and he was tired.

And confused.

He surveyed the scene, taking in the tall man with his head bowed to the table, his weasely-looking companion. The naked hunger he'd seen in the faces of the men the instant he'd entered the Inn was now restrained, but it was still there, simmering, waiting. Waiting for what?

The Slinger turned his black eyes back to the woman, "Is there a room I can have?"

"Not in this town," she answered looking at him and the huskiness was still there, in her voice. "Perhaps you can try the stable."

The Slinger allowed a tight smile to play on his face and the woman's eyes, seeing it, glinted with greed. "Surely there must be a place."

"You could try my place stranger," A man behind and to his far right said. "It's small and a little uncomfortable but-"

"You butt out of this McQuaid! You have a wife and three kids and there's hardly enough room for you now," the woman's eyes flared as she spoke.

The man called McQuaid looked a little uncertain. He was round-eyed with short, oily hair, going prematurely grey and he was unshaven. His mind weighed the advantage of some silver against the longer-term benefits he could lose. He looked away. There were hidden smiles on the faces of some of the other men in the Inn and McQuaid shuffled his feet and glowered into the glass in front of him.

"There could be a place," the woman said to the Slinger.

"Where?"

"There's a price involved," she looked coyly at him.

"Isn't there always?" the Slinger finished the last of the water in his glass. He now felt hungry and tired. The offer was not without its attraction.

At the back of his mind, through the mists of confusion, he thought of the traitor. He had made it this far, but the man was still ahead of him. It could be that a trap had been laid here for him.

The blond man's machinations had slowed him down before when he'd got close to him, but he preferred not to think about that now. He had controlled his body too long, made sacrifices that demanded respite and he was impossibly tired and with scant control left. "Where's this room?" he asked.

There was total silence and the woman smiled, her eyes glittered seductively in the Inn's dancing torch lights. "Come back in two hours," she said "closing time." The Slinger nodded and walked out, his heels hardly made a sound on the Inn's hard-packed earthen floor.

Behind him, as he left, the Inn exploded into a babble of raised voices.

The Slinger's steps took him to the one place in town he knew the blond man would have to visit: The stables. The blond man had a powerful steed and he had taken good care of it throughout the desert crossing, walking rather than riding it.

The Slinger knew that the distance between them was closing and even with the desert behind him, the traitor would not be able to pick up full speed for some time yet.

Maybe, just maybe, there was yet hope.

The stable-master was fat and unshaven. He was the first person in the town the Slinger saw wearing a kimono. It was soiled at the front, as if he'd spent weeks vomiting on it, and as dirt-encrusted as the Slinger's clothes. Around the stable-master's thick neck hang a bluestone amulet. The bottom of his kimono was heavy with clumps of dried horse-dung.

The Slinger took all this in at a glance. A wizened old woman dressed in the worn, faded, clothes of a Lady of the Reading sat on a half-barrel outside the stable. Her eyes, milky with cataracts, turned to the direction of the Slinger's steps.

"A Reading sir, a Reading young sir. Would you like a Reading?"

There was a stench emanating from the entire place.

"Shut up you old crone!" the stable-master said and he swung his foot back aiming a kick at her. Halfway through the swing his shoulder was gripped by the Slinger's gloved hand, he was pulled off balance and turned around to face the jet-black eyes glistening with the promise of blood.

"Let her be," the Slinger said and the stable-master's insolent composure instantly crumpled.

"I'm sorry your Highness! I'm sorry! I didn't know. I only wanted to please your Highness. Save you the trouble-" he curtsied quickly, head bent towards the filth-covered ground in submission.

"You have displeased me," the Slinger said and the stable master blanched.

"Your Highness, I-"

"I need a horse. A good one. See that I get it."

With that the Slinger pushed the fat man away. He stumbled on a stone, caught his balance in time to prevent his body from sprawling in the filth and turned and bowed once more quickly to the Slinger. "Your Highness, thank you. Thank you." he said, bowing each time and he retreated towards the dark doorway of the stinking stables. "A horse your Highness. Of course, a horse. Thank you, thank you."

The old woman cackled at the stable-master's discomfiture. The Slinger looked after where the stable- master had gone with an expressionless look on his face. He had wanted to avoid this happening at all costs.

He had not yet fully recovered from his descent from the spirals and his control on his temper was still lax. The stable-master's behaviour had angered him beyond his current capacity for restraint. It also had verified his fears. There was no law here. Had not been for some time.

The blond man must have found fertile ground. The Slinger suddenly knew he would have to be on his guard.

"A Reading young sir?"

He turned to the old woman. She had stopped cackling and her sightless eyes were turned his way.

"A Reading madam," he agreed gravely and there was silence. An unexpected tear appeared at the corner of one ruined eye and slowly trickled down the withered old cheek. She bit her bottom lip to stop it trembling.

"Forgive me young master. It's been a long- . A Reading then." Her hands disappeared under her robe and she brought out a copy of The Book. It was bound in leather, scuffed and weathered from much use and the gold leaf that had marked the yin and yang characters on the cover had faded long ago.

She put The Book on her lap, clutched the yarrow stalks in one hand as if to make sure they were all there and then and she began twirling them from one hand to the other. "State your question," she said and there was a ceremonial officiousness in her voice.

"I have stated it," the Slinger said.

The wrinkled hands continued their game, the yarrow stalks twirled. Slowly, the hexagram began falling out. It was number eighteen.

The Slinger knew it well. within the haze of his slow mind the words sprang up like flames of fire: *Disruption!*

The Slinger knelt in the dust in front of it. He could almost hear voices past calling out the Reading: *Disruption leads to great success. It is worthwhile crossing great rivers. Three days before, three days after.*

He linked the sacred words of the Reading with the associated image he had been taught during the years he'd spent training in the Butokuden, the Great Hall: *There is wind under a mountain, disrupted. Cultured people inspire others to develop virtue.*

He thought it made some sense. He'd just crossed the desert: A river of sand. It had taken more than three days but time had no meaning in the Oracle's eyes. He was going to catch the blond man.

"Thank you madam," he bowed to the old woman and put four silver coins in the palm of her hand and closed the wrinkled fingers round them.

"You're not of the People," she said suddenly and he looked up surprised.

"No,"

"You seek somebody."

"A traitor."

"Then you know the Oracle. You have been warned. Do not dally here."

"Has the man I seek been here?"

"I did not see him come, but men like him leave a lingering trail behind. The Oracle sensed it, it spoke to me, told me to come here."

"Do you know where he's gone?"

"The Oracle says he's travelling North, to the mountains."

The Slinger stood up. His gloved hand went into a pocket and came out with a silver star. It was highly polished, the engraved dragon emblem shone on it. He carefully pinned it to his chest, just over the heart.

There was no point in hiding his identity any more. He had been unmasked. The star of the Slingers shining on his chest spelled out its message clear for all to see: Law reaches everywhere.

"I am in your debt," he said to the old woman gravely and she waved a dried-up bony hand at him.

She put The Book away. "Be on your guard," she whispered at his retreating footsteps.

***

The Ronin, woman from the bar moved quietly. She showed him into a dark, musty room. There was the clutter of furniture everywhere. A large bookcase covered in dust, the books obviously unread, a small table, next to a bigger one, chairs.

One side of the room was dominated by a large double bed. Her main place of business.

The woman moved to the bed and started undressing. In the twilight the scars threading their way over her left shoulder and onto her back were invisible.

"No," the Slinger said stopping her nimble fingers in mid-motion, "I am hungry. First I must eat."

The woman let out a sigh of impatience but stopped shedding her clothes. Half-undressed, her small breasts bouncing lightly in time with her step, she vanished into a small alcove off the big room. The Slinger heard the clutter of metal pots and presently the smell of red beans and corn cooking reached his nostrils.

He felt his mouth salivating. He was hungry. It made thinking very difficult, this weakness of the body. He had to learn to control it again. His adversary, protected by the spells of attrition he wove, suffered of no such defects and if he was to defeat him he had to rise to similar heights of imperviousness.

As he stood, waiting for his food, looking at the dusty, shabby furniture and pondering what it represented, night fell outside. The woman brought a small candle, on a candle-holder of enriched tin, exquisitely curved.

"No more light," she said and the Slinger nodded. He looked at the scars on her back.

The deep marks of the scourge.

"What is your name?" he asked as she put a plate of hot food on the big table, a big tumbler of crystal-clear water next to it, a rust coloured earthen jug of sake next to that.

She motioned for him to sit down.

"Letitia," she answered his question. She met his eyes with no effort to cover herself. Her breasts stood out all proud, their dark nippled tips erect in the chill of the gloom.

Her nakedness was like a challenge to him. The visible scars that announced her punishment for her crimes cried out now for some response.

The Slinger said nothing.

He returned his attention to the plate she'd put in front of him and began to eat in silence. He shovelled the food in efficient, quick bursts of motion as she watched.

He was methodical, chewing each mouthful as if he wanted to extract every last ounce of sustenance from it. Presently he finished what was in front of him and, ignoring the sake, reached for the jug of water. The clear liquid sparkled in the candle's golden light.

He poured himself a glass and drunk deeply. He then filled it again.

"You were hungry," Letitia said, watching him still.

The flame of the candle made the shadows jump across her naked upper body. The skin glistened, brown and taut. Her breasts and erect nipples invited further attention.

The Slinger stood up and let his eyed play over her again, more slowly this time.

The expression Letitia saw in them made her shiver. She brought her hands up across her chest the delicate fingers cupping and shielding each breast. Standing there, like this, she looked like an avatar of seduction.

There was an air of wounded vulnerability about her. The atmosphere of captive sexuality was further accentuated by the long, straight, black tresses that came over her shoulders and chest and barely hid the upper slopes of her exquisite breasts. The thin wisps of fabric that still kept her dress up, at her waist completed the picture.

The Slinger seemed to teeter on indecision, his eyes unable to move away from her available body and then, as all restraints he'd tried to put in place were suddenly swept away by fatigue and mad desire, he reached for her, swept her up into his arms and she (playing her role to perfection) let out a cry of surprise at his roughness, mixed with pain, and triumph.

It was a cry she was to repeat many times that night as he lifted her and threw her onto the big, double bed, her body crashed vigourously beneath his own.

His skilled hands already moving on the surface of her skin ready to inflict, in equal measure, pleasure and pain.

***

"Are you really a Star-Slinger?" Letitia looked at the big silver badge pinned to the Slinger's black tunic. She was dressed in a sheer, silk gown split at the side, to reveal the ripe, smooth line of her thighs. The morning sun filtered through the broken shutters in dust-clogged rays of light and drew the Slinger's attention to the motes of dust swirling in the musty air of the girl's room.

Lying in bed, eyeing her, the Slinger faintly nodded his answer to her question. He seemed lost in concentration.

"Then you must have come after the blond man on the pale horse. The one who was here before you,"

The Slinger looked up, "Did you sleep with him too?"

"No. I would have liked to, but he had no money. Nothing to give me but advice," she laughed. "He held court in the Inn. He gave everyone advice and he blessed the farmers laying down the new crop and the two pregnant women. And then he left. Didn't even stay a day."

"How long ago was that?"

"Two days before you came. Maybe three." she looked to see what his reaction would be to her deliberate vagueness.

The Slinger remained impassive. Only three days, he thought. Three days. That's all the lead he had. He thought of the words of the Oracle: *Three days before, three days after.* Three days after what? The desert crossing had slowed the blond man down and he must be getting desperate. Whatever magical powers he possessed, the crossing of distances seemed to weaken him. Every time the Slinger got nearer he felt his confidence in the sufficiency of his own abilities grow.

I can defeat him, the Slinger thought to himself. I can defeat him, I can defeat him, I can defeat him. It was his own personal mantra. The thought had sustained him in the difficult times when Time had changed for him, just before the desert crossing and the dream had claimed him. The shadows of his ancestors had assisted him even then, had shown him the way out of the murkiness he'd found himself caught up in. But he had lost so much. There was so much to reclaim.

He stood up and reached for his clothes.

"You must pay," Letitia said and the Slinger smiled. From a pocket of his tunic he took out two silver coins and placed them on the small side table by the bed, balanced one on top of the other.

"That's not enough."

"It is, for now."

The Slinger dressed quickly, all visible traces of fatigue gone from his movements, and went outside.

The townsfolk avoided him. There was a loaded silence every time his eyes met theirs and they quickly looked away and hurried past him.

He could sympathise with the resentment, even understand it. Here he was, a Star-Slinger, and he wasn't even of the People. Whatever else his star and swords announced to the world, his round eyes told a different story.

Be it as it may, he had no time to make converts now. The night's abundant lovemaking and the deep sleep he'd drifted in had stripped the inertia induced by the desert crossing from his body. He felt ready to move again.

He asked a young man chopping cord wood at the back of one of the ramshackle houses where he could find the Lady of the Reading and the young man looked shifty and scratched his head and said he didn't know.

The Slinger pretended to believe him.

He left the dusty streets behind and skirted the town and the pathetic fields of crop. The stunted corn and beanstalks lay wilting under the harsh sun, this close to the desert, no produce had much chance of healthy fruition unless a lot of water was provided for it and even then, the soil was too thin and too badly eroded to sustain any kind of farming for long.

With his customary patience the Slinger spent long hours examining the iron-hard earth, to the North of the town: the road the blond man had taken.

He picked up the faint traces of the now familiar horseshoe imprints quickly and he followed them for an hour, until they faded. The blond man was using his spells again, like he had done in the desert. The Slinger knew that before long the blond man would tire and the traces would appear again. It puzzled him that the blond man went to such lengths to cover his tracks.

Ever since he had followed him, the blond man's route had been unwavering. The traces pointed due North before they vanished.

The Slinger returned to the town.

He thought that the town must have a name and he looked carefully for it but could not find it posted anywhere. He spent the rest of the day in Letitia's room, above the Inn, listening to the muffled sound of voices that floated up to him and the occasional burst of coarse laughter.

Once he thought that he heard female screams but he ignored them and the sound stopped and did not repeat itself.

Whatever damage the desert had done to him was fading fast. He decided to buy a horse as soon as possible and leave the town. He'd been here for two days already and he could feel his sense of unease grow like an itch under his skin.

At night Letitia cooked a plate of the red beans that seemed to be the staple diet here and then, later, gave him her body to use again. This time she asked no money for it and when the morning light bled through the shutters again, the Slinger woke to find her clinging to him, her head on his chest, her long black hair wound round his neck, like a noose.

Letitia didn't open the Inn that day and she took off the earrings marking her as available. "You are more than enough at the moment, they'll have to manage without me," she'd said as explanation and the Slinger had only looked at her in expressionless silence.

He wasn't sure he understood all that was happening to him but he felt the urgency to leave intensify in his breast. The words of the Oracle troubled him and he thought perhaps he should consult the Lady of the Reading again.

At noon Letitia made the bed. She changed into a sheer peach coloured gown and waited for him to join her. From a pocket of his clothes, the Slinger produced a folded map, made of soft leather, and spread it open on the bed.

"You're leaving," Letitia said and her voice was flat and colourless. There was nothing the Slinger could say to her. He undressed slowly, his eyes scanning the map while he was doing so, looking at the patch representing the large tract of desert he'd just come across. There were tiny dots with names scrawled beside them, marking the edges of the desert: border towns.

"What's the name of this town?" the Slinger asked.

"It doesn't have one. It's just the town," Letitia shrugged her pretty shoulders and the Slinger snorted in unfeigned disgust. Ronin, he thought, savages, what could you expect?

He was out of his clothes now and the sight of his body, lean and smooth, with hard, clearly defined muscle moving just beneath the skin, aroused Letitia's passion.

On hands and knees, the top of her gown falling open to give him a generous view of her pointed breasts, she moved across the bed, reaching for him. "Who needs names?" she purred. Her words were followed by a slight creak outside the door, wooden planks shifting under sudden weight.

It was all the warning the Slinger needed. He was used to deciphering noises. His training had left nothing to chance.

He turned round just as the flimsy wooden door was kicked open and the tall man he'd encountered in the Inn when he first entered the town, rushed in. He was clutching his knife in both hands, arms held high overhead and his mouth was open in a noiseless scream.

The other man, the round-eyes: McQuaid, was right behind him, an old muzzle-loader held across his chest.

The Slinger fell back on the bed on the face of the heavier man's charge. He caught the double handed blow on crossed wrists, twisted them in a sharp scissor motion and watched the knife clatter to the floor as the big man's wrist bones broke with a brittle crack.

In the same motion the Slinger shoved the man's body aside, placing it halfway between the armed McQuaid and himself.

McQuaid had the gun ready now and was bringing it up to bear when the Slinger kicked out. The ball of his foot caught the gun-barrel and pushed it up towards the ceiling where it harmlessly discharged its load. Before McQuaid could recover from the instinctive blink of the gun-blast, the Slinger was upon him.

With a movement that was almost graceful he brought the edge of his rigid palm against McQuaid's collar-bone. Letitia let out a choked cry and brought her hands to her mouth as she heard the sharp crack of the bone breaking.

McQuaid fell to his knees with a groan. He dropped the gun on the floor. His left arm hang down useless. His right hand clutched the shoulder where the bone had broken. Spittle lined his lips and he was suddenly very pale.

The Slinger looked at McQuaid, pointed to the tall man who was sitting on the floor hugging his shattered wrists to his big body and rocking back and forth in shock.

There was a vacant look in the big man's eyes and his mouth emitted a moaning that reminded the Slinger of water buffalos mating. "Get him out of here," he said and McQuaid scrambled to obey, his ashen face screwed up with pain.

The door shut behind them. The hole in the roof and the smell of gunpowder were the only signs of their having been there. The Slinger picked up the big, heavy gun. Its barrel was still hot. He propped it up against the wall, by the door.

"You didn't have to hurt them," Letitia pouted at him. Her face was uncertain. "They were only jealous. They can no longer afford-"

She never finished her sentence.

With a blurred motion the Slinger reached out and ripped the sheer gown from her body.

The adrenalin charge of the fight made his every nerve-end tingle and he was already massively erect. Without a word he threw her on the bed forced her legs apart and violently plunged himself into her. He felt his mind consumed by a mindless anger that only barely matched the fire of lust that gripped his body.

Her cries of passion were the most satisfying sounds he'd heard for a long time.

Afterwards, she watched him as he dressed. There was a clinking as he put on his tunic and she perked up.

The Slinger frowned, checked something on the inside of it and fastened a loop. "You've been through this," he said and she gave him her pouty look in reply. He moved the tunic from side to side satisfied that there was no clinking, this time.

"What are they? Those strange looking stars?"

"They are not your concern," the Slinger said.

He turned to leave. His back was to her and she sat up on the bed, totally nude and said to him: "The blond man said that you'd have them. He warned us about you,"

The Slinger stopped and slowly turned. What he heard in her voice was

disappointment, anger and sorrow mixed with fear. He recognized his mistake now in allowing his body to entrap him like this. The woman's presence had taken the edge off his faculties. He'd made too many mistakes already and he was as much to blame for this as the effect of the desert. The Oracle had spoken of three days. This was the third. He was going to take no more chances, he decided, he had to go. Had to go now.

"What sort of warnings?"

"He held court in the Inn. Told us of evils to come. He said there's growing violence and the world is in the grip of Disruption. He said there will be an end to our time of idyl and warned that the devil will come walking out of the desert bearing the star and that devil must be punished!"

"I must go."

It was already too late. As he had feared he'd stayed too long. Visibly shaken, the Slinger opened the door, stepped out into the blazing sunlight, descended the steps that led to the dusty street below, surveying it all the while for visible signs of danger.

Seeing how her words had affected him Letitia gathered the bedsheets around her naked body. Trailing them on the dusty wooden floor she followed him to the open doorway.

"He spoke of corrupt Lawmakers. Do you hear? Corrupt!" she shouted at his back and the Slinger stared straight ahead and made for the stables. The street was totally empty.

And still her voice followed him, shrill with emotion. "He gave us a sign. He said the desert shall lead our fight against corruption. The desert shall take you! You devil-spawn! The desert shall punish you!"

Presently there was the sound of muffled, hysterical, weeping, receding with each step he took. The Slinger approached the stables, alert for trouble, his eyes squinting against the pitiless glare thrown up by the white street-dust. He wished he'd paid greater heed to the words of the Oracle now and left before the three days were up, but the Oracle had strange notions of time. It did not reckon days by the standard of humans and his body had been weakened beyond control.

He figured he'd paid the price for *gaffla*. His only hope now was that the price was not his life.

There was the creaking of a door somewhere in front of him and the

Slinger stopped.

The stable master appeared out of the deep shade of the stables, a fat woman as broad as she was tall and dressed in dirty black hovered close behind him.

The stable-master still wore the filthy kimono.

"Is my horse ready?" the Slinger asked.

The stable-master looked at the woman and seemed to draw courage from her presence. He turned to face the Slinger. There was a flash of movement behind them and a young child with a dirt-encrusted face ran from the stable. It dodged past the fat woman and between the stable master's legs and stood to one side. It leaned against the far barn wall and stared openly at the Slinger.

The child could not have been more than twelve, though it was short for its age. It pointed at the Slinger with a dirt-encrusted finger and yelled: "Devil!"

The woman brought both her hands to touch the centre of her forehead. She held a bluestone amulet firmly in them. Her gaze was riveted on the Slinger and her lips moved fervently in silent prayer.

"Devil!" repeated the child.

"There'll be no horse for you here," the stable-master found the courage to say at last but his voice was unsteady. The Slinger put his hand on the hilt of his sword. The short one, worn at his waist.

"All the horses are gone. They escaped this morning," said the stable-master quickly. "The stable's empty," he took a step back and moved aside to gesture at the open stable door. Impenetrable darkness reigned beyond the door. All was silent. "Look for yourself if you like," the stable-master said and the Slinger felt sick, deep inside himself.

Was this to be the traitor's trap? Was he to be given no chance to escape it?

Keeping his eyes on the stable door and the three people in front of him the Slinger started moving backwards. One step at a time.

He'd almost rounded the corner, made it into the dirt path that led across the main street from where he could reach Letitia's Inn when the little boy cried out: "The desert! The desert! The desert is coming for him!"

Its dirty finger pointed over the Slinger's left shoulder, at an angle aimed at the sky.

The Slinger turned.

There was a towering funnel of spinning hot air, darkening fast, moving towards them. An unearthly wail rose from it and where it hovered, just off the ground, from the gaps between the houses the Slinger could see a cloud of dust and sand that swirled and turned and glowing particles moved in and out of it.

It was almost upon them.

The Slinger heard the heavy footfall behind him and turned just in time to avoid the pitchfork aimed at him, held by the stable-master. His left hand shot out, followed the momentum of his body and the stiff edge of his palm caught the fat man on the throat, beneath the droop of his pendulous chin.

There was the crumpling sound of cartilage and the stable-master went down, a terrible gurgling issued from his lips. The Slinger turned, looked for a place to run to, but it was too late.

Howling devilishly the tornado tore through the town, cutting two smaller buildings to the left of the Inn in half. It fed on loose planks of wood and broken glass and anything it could find, arming itself, and as it crossed the main street, the blond man's trap was finally sprung.

Ignoring the terrible wind and the sand and dust and the deadly debris that flew through the air, the townsfolk swarmed out of their houses, armed with knives and axes and rocks and thick logs of wood. Men and women and children, both round-eyes and of the People, formed a tight knot, and they all closed in, on the Slinger.

The Slinger drew his long sword and cartwheeled his body away from them, twirling in a blurred motion of black-covered flesh and shining steel and one of the bolder ones rushed in to strike him, trying to intercept the spinning body, and the Slinger lashed out.

The sword cut through the soft flesh and bone and arteries and severed the man's head from his body, so that it flew in a bright red arc through the air and rolled away from him and stopped at the feet of the advancing mob, the eyes caught open and staring still.

The wind howled behind them then and they all screamed with madness. The blond man's power and the strange spell of the desert, strong now in them.

The Slinger had gained some distance now. Had put a good space between himself and the mob. He knelt and his hands reached inside a fold of his jacket and he pulled out two of the four pointed stars Letitia had admired, the points sharpened and glistening wickedly and his hands were a blur as he flung them at the moving mass of bodies and a woman went down, one of the stars firmly embedded in the edge of an eye, and a man stumbled and fell, clutching his throat.

They threw things at him now, stones and wood and the wind was about them and glass swirled through the air and the Slinger drew out two long slender blades and sent them into the massed bodies and two more people fell and others tripped over them.

A long piece of glass carried by the wind cut across the back of his thigh and the pain made him grunt with surprise and momentarily stop and a stone caught him on the side of the head and he felt blood well out of the cut. He isolated the sense of pain and as he did so his clothes were tugged by the howling wind and sand and dirt obscured his vision and made breathing difficult.

In desperation he threw one last blade into the mass of bodies and somebody went down, clutching his chest and then they had closed the gap and were suddenly all around him, within easy killing distance.

The Slinger drew the shorter sword and met them as he'd been trained, a blade in each hand and he was a fury of motion, a demon of steel. He whirled in the midst of them and his blades reached out and flicked, picking hands off female arms, slashing across haggard, drawn faces with mad, glazed eyes, cutting a wide swath through them.

He moved across the street and they followed him still, maddened hyenas worrying a lion, leaving dead bodies to mark the trail behind, and the Slinger facing them, both hands moving blurringly fast began to retreat up the steps of Letitia's Inn.

The double doors behind him swung open and McQuaid came out holding a knife, right arm up in the air, his left arm in a sling, and the Slinger twisted his body sideways and his long sword suddenly thrust backwards and impaled him. McQuaid died without making a sound.

It was the first thrust he'd been forced to make, but it was enough. It slowed him down as he pulled the sword out and it gave them time to close in on him. A child clung to his legs, its whole weight on his knees and he stumbled and fell.

He let go of the long sword, slipped out a knife and began stubbing about him, twisting and rolling his body on the floor to make it harder for them to find their mark.

Writhing like this, he rolled into the Inn, twisting between the tables and chairs, with all of them following.

An old woman fell heavily on top of him and he stabbed her in the back of the neck, withdrew his blade quickly to pierce the breast of a boy that was coming at him with a stone held high in one small hand.

There was the burning of pain as somebody pushed a sliver of glass into him, in his left arm, and he turned and stabbed the young girl that had done it, in the throat, under the chin, pushing his blade up into her brain.

There were too many of them. Their blood flowed freely but they still kept coming, howling, throwing themselves on his knife. He kicked out with both feet now, lashing out, and felt the bone-crushing impact as the heels of his boots connected with somebody's chest and he once more rolled away from the melee of bodies, towards his long sword and somebody called out his name.

It surprised him long enough, to receive a knife thrust in the back, high on the left shoulder-blade. It was the deepest wound he suffered and the pain spasmed his body, whipped him into a new frenzy and he jack-knifed, his right leg swept out the legs from under his assailant, a young man in his early twenties, and his left arm wrapped itself under his chin, pushing the head back as he fell, to expose the carotid, which he severed with a flash-like motion.

He paused to bend down and pick up his sword and then he fled, through the door. The bodies and blood and the confusion he'd created slowed down the mad mob behind him and outside Letitia was dragging two horses, her long black hair whipped about by the wind, her eyes screwed tight and a hand held up to shield them from the sand and the dust.

"Get on!" she shouted and he vaulted on the saddle and under cover of the dust they rode out of the town, leaving the wailing wind to die out behind them and the surviving townsfolk to recover from their craze and bury the dead.

***

Chapter 2

The Weeping Demon

The blond man's trail went due North and the Slinger instinctively followed it. The wasteland spread all round them, behind them lay the desert and the nameless town, filled with its grieving and its dead.

They rode for hours, beneath the merciless sun, pushing the horses as hard as they dared, using the last of the water Letitia had taken with her, drinking from their water flasks while still on the trot.

Twice, Letitia looked back to see if the whirling pillar of wind would follow them and when she asked the Slinger about it he simply said that magic did not work that way and would say no more.

The sun was beginning to dip towards the horizon when they came upon a pile of rocks, protruding out of the hard ground like broken bones pushed through flesh and the Slinger signalled for them to stop. They reined the horses in and Letitia looked questioningly at him.

The Slinger looked at the baked earth, his eyes following the barely perceptible markings pressed in the soil. "He's been here, but he didn't stay long." He said. Letitia said nothing and the Slinger drew himself to his full height on his saddle and looked all around them.

In the failing light, he spotted at the edge of the horizon the straight bar-lines thrown by the shadows of trees and he knew that there would be a farmhouse found there.

He'd only just recovered from the desert crossing and he didn't want to risk another trip up the spirals and the unpredictable price *gaffla* would take. Not with the woman riding with him. He was hungry and thirsty again and his wounds needed seeing to.

"There," he said and he pointed and Letitia strained to see. There was a feint plume of smoke rising gently in the immobile air before it was broken into a swirl by the spiralling thermals, and was scattered.

They slowed the horses down, giving them time to rest.

"How did you know my name?" he asked Letitia. It was the first time he'd spoken to her directly since she'd saved his life in the town and she had been waiting for it.

"The old woman told it me. When I went to round up the horses from the back of the stables. She told me your name was Yame."

"What else did she say?"

"She seemed to know a lot about you. She told me to hurry. She said that you know Disruption has not yet began."

"Why did you save me?"

"I want to ride with you."

"Why?"

"There was nothing for me back there. You saw them. You're a Star-Slinger. After sleeping with you my value as a courtesan wouldn't safeguard my life long,"

Her answers seemed to satisfy him and he nodded to himself. His face was completely inscrutable, his long black hair flowed unbound to his shoulders and danced as he rode. Letitia thought that she hadn't seen him wear the hood Slingers wore since the day he'd first walked into town and into her Inn.

They reached the trees just before darkness fell. There was a farmhouse nestled amongst them, just as the Slinger knew there would be. In a plot, next to it, golden spears of corn reached for the sky.

There were chickens and hens, running in for the night roost and two smaller buildings at the back of the house, protected from the worst of the wind and the bite of the dust, gave off subtle smells that spoke of animal husbandry and well cared-for livestock.

The entire place had the well-kept look that marked hard work, the coin with which one etched a living from this unforgiving soil, and the Slinger advanced into the courtyard with confidence. In the dying twilight the silver star on his chest stood out against the black of his clothes.

"Peace to you,"

The Slinger stopped, turned to his right where a man stood in a ditch. The man was in late youth and the ditch rose to his chest. Dried sweat had streaked his face with dust and he held some sort of double-bladed digging implement in his hands. As he spoke, he put the implement down and climbed out of the ditch.

"And to you," the Slinger replied.

The man walked up to them and without being asked, took the reins of their horses in one hand. "Water is there," he pointed to a cairn of stones on the left side of the farmhouse. Stone steps descended into the earth and the sound of water trickling reached their ears.

The Slinger dismounted, motioned for Letitia to do the same. He looked around the place. "Get some water," he ordered the woman, "see that the horses are fed."

"You're a Star-Slinger," the man looked at the badge pinned to the Slinger's chest. The latter made no reply.

"Do you mean to pay?"

"For the water and our food. A night's sleep under your roof, some supplies if you can spare them,"

"Yet you're the Law,"

"The Law pays too, same as everyone else."

The man scratched his head. "I'll tell my wife to prepare some food," he said "and some hot water."' he cast a meaningful look at the Slinger's stained clothing, the holes in the fabric round where the blood had dried black and the flesh featured torn, red and bruised, "You seem to have come in from a long ride."

The Slinger followed the young farmer inside the low-roofed building. He felt detached from his body, cut-off, his imperfect memory clouded with freshly-perpetrated scenes of death. Something had happened back at the nameless town. Something momentous.

Something invisible and all-pervading that went beyond the pain and the death he had been forced to inflict upon the townsfolk.

He wished he could remember the blond man's name. His nature. But all was dark inside his mind.

"My wife," the young farmer shattered his thoughts, forced his attention back to the present. "She will see to your clothes."

The Slinger bowed his head without speaking and the young farmer turned and walked back out of the farmhouse.

The man's wife was a lot younger than he, strong, pretty and vibrant. Unlike her husband she wasn't of the People. She had long blonde hair that she'd coiled in a tight bun on her head and her eyes were the colour of the sky in Summer. Her figure was ripe and full, her young bosom straining at the front of her dress, her hips not yet pushed out by childbirth.

She waited patiently, her back turned, while the Slinger took off his clothes and removed all his armoury from the dozen catch-pockets and folds within them and wrapped himself in the rough, woolen blanket she'd handed him.

She bent to pick up his clothes from where he'd dropped them. "I'll see these are washed," she said simply and her voice was as young and vibrant as she was and its sound touched off hidden chords, deep within the Slinger and his frame within the blanket tensed with forgotten pain.

Before he could say a word, Letitia arrived, face washed clean, the sleeves of her dress rolled up to the elbows "I've filled the water flasks-" she began and then stopped eyes flashing as she took in the simple pretty face of the farmer's wife. Her eyes shot back to the Slinger, the woollen blanket he held closed in front with one hand. "I see you're busy," there was a heavy edge to her voice. A grating that sent goosebumps all over the Slinger's body.

"No," he said. He turned to face her. Out of the corner of his eye he saw the farmer's wife finish picking up his clothes and silently retreat. A moment had been lost here, he thought. A chance to learn something of the past. "Come on inside. The darkness will bring cold."

***

The farmer's wife set a simple meal for the two travellers, herself and her husband and a large pot of water to boil over the hearth fire.

The Slinger and Letitia ate heartily the simple fare of beans and black bread and roasted corn. They washed it down with farm-made wine. It tasted cleanly of the spring and the earth. "It's the spring," the farmer explained "that water makes everything taste good. Just couldn't survive without it."

The inside of the farmhouse was strewn with straw. The floor was hard-packed earth covered with rough hewn slabs of stone. There were three rooms in the farmhouse. One was a bedroom, the other a storeroom. They were all sitting down eating their meal in the third.

"You're welcome to stay for as long as you want," the farmer's wife said during the meal.

"We can't stay long," the Slinger spoke over his food. He ate with care as if each mouthful was to be prized and he never drank without swallowing first. "We are days behind," and he noticed the quick look that was exchanged between the farmer and his wife.

"The weather will remain dry for months," the farmer said, "it'll be hard travelling on the way. The springs are no longer what they used to be. Things have changed."

The Slinger nodded in ascent. His black eyes, lit by the dancing flames shone like burning embers. "Things have changed."

"There used to be a village here." The farmer said. "A small community. They left when the raids began. We were the only ones to stay."

"Why?"

The farmer hesitated. "The Law never touched us before. We believed we could live without it."

"The Law touches everybody."

"Not here."

"Even here."

A long silence followed the Slinger's words. The farmer's wife kept her eyes firmly on the table. Her bottom lip trembled as if she was holding back tears.

"Why are you here Slinger?" the farmer said at last.

The Slinger looked up, eyes missing nothing, his mind struggling to make sense of all he was reading here. This was no trap, he was certain of that, yet the blond man had passed through here. Something wrenched, deep inside his breast, and he had to swallow hard to clear his throat. Why, really was he here? The answer that sprang to his lips hid all his doubts: "I am the Law." It was said like a challenge, but the farmer smiled grimly and said nothing more. His wife stood up to clear the table and bring them more wine.

Throughout the meal Letitia remained silent.

Neither the farmer nor his wife addressed her directly and the Slinger simply ignored her.

When the farmer and his wife retired, she looked sullenly at the Slinger sitting cross-legged, in front of the open fire. There was a pot of boiling water brought in by the farmer's wife, lying on the floor, at his feet.

The Slinger had shed the blanket that had covered him and now sat totally naked, his swords by his side. The dancing firelight revealed the skin of his body bruised and broken in a dozen places. There was a deep, ugly wound on his left shoulder-blade weeping still a thin, watery red and there were dozens of minor gushes on his legs, chest and arms.

As she watched he opened a small cloth sack he'd removed from his clothes and took out some of its contents and put them in the boiling water. Immediately, a delicate fragrance filled the room. Letitia sniffed loudly. The Slinger continued to ignore her.

He stirred the pot with his fingers and watched the water change colour to a deep, muddy brown. He took a clean scrap of cloth and dipped it in the mud-coloured water and rubbed it over his body, gently washing over the cuts. His sharp intake of breath told her it hurt him.

At last Letitia could stand his silence no longer.

She went over to him.

"Can I do your back?" she asked, and without waiting for a reply she took the cloth from his hand and gently applied it over the cuts on his body.

Wherever the wet cloth touched the dried blood-clots dissolved. The Slinger's body went rigid with pain each time a deep wound was bathed, the hard muscles clearly defined beneath the white skin, and

Letitia took a perverse satisfaction from this show of the pain she was inflicting upon him. Stripped of the perfection of his lovemaking and the remorselessness of his killing techniques, to her, he now seemed at last human and vulnerable.

When she was finished she dragged the bedding the farmer's wife had provided near the fire, spread the blanket over the straw floor and used her clothes to fashion a pillow for him.

The Slinger lay on his back, breathing quietly.

As she watched, the mantle of pain that had made him seem more human receded from his body, and he assumed his cold, impassive demeanour again. He reached out and unsheathed his long sword with a fluid, practised motion and brought the blade close to his face, turning it this way and that to catch the firelight.

"What are you doing?" Letitia asked.

He surprised her by answering. "Talking to it. It listens."

He sounded as if he meant it.

Without turning his eyes away, his left hand vanished into another little cloth bag and when it came out it held a thick pad of white silk, lightly wet with something. Gently, almost lovingly he began to rub it along the edge of the long sword. A low guttural sound came from his throat every time he did it and the sound grated on Letitia's nerves and made the hair at the base of her neck stand up on edge.

"I don't like that woman." she said at last to break the silence, "The way her round eyes look at you."

The Slinger's face had an inward, peaceful look and her words drew involuntary laughter from his lips. "There's nothing I can offer her she hasn't already got," he said and looked up at the ceiling. Great thick beams crossed overhead. "Why didn't the blond man sleep with you?" he asked suddenly and caught off guard, Letitia drew in her breath sharply. Her eyes filled with horror and panic and her hands bunched into fists at her throat.

Unerringly he'd hit upon his mark: "What did he see in you that made him spurn you?"

Letitia whimpered, fell to her knees in front of the fire. The Slinger kept his eyes riveted to the ceiling as he spoke.

The balm was doing its potent work and there was a new peace in him now. He was drawing tendrils of emotion, seeing Letitia with the eyes of the newly released from respite. A part of him thought that the desert crossing had changed him, stripped him of his old identity so that he was born anew.

He let the thought die undeveloped, he was too tired and sleepy to chase it.

His new awareness though did not rest at that. It focussed his attention on his actions since the desert crossing. Replayed for him the scenes of carnage he'd created in the nameless town. He was directly responsible for that carnage, he knew that now, there was guilt building inside him, and he would have to deal with it in time.

But first he must find out about Letitia.

"What was it he said to you that made you follow me?"

"Please, please," she whimpered.

"Why did you save me Letitia?"

"Please," she was begging openly now and there were tears filling her eyes. "Don't send me away, please. I'll tell you. He read my palm. All of us. Everyone in the town.I didn't want to but he made the men hold me down, held my hand up to the light. Hesaid he saw death. He saw me drowning under waves unless I followed my heart."

"Waves in the desert," he mused "Why did you save me?"

"Look at me!" she cried out "I am Ronin, Outcast, scourged in public. It was that town or nowhere. Sleep with the men or die etching a living at the bar, growing haggard and old and fat like their women. Do you understand now? Do you understand?"

The Slinger gave her no answer. The balm he'd put on his wounds had mixed with the wine in his belly and his eyes had shut. His sword lay across his chest, the white pad of silk he'd held had slipped out of his fingers. His chest rose and fell evenly. Letitia pulled herself up to him and gently prised the sword out of his grip. She expected him to wake up then but when he didn't move she placed it by his side and fiercely hugged his naked body.

"I had nothing in the world before," she said to his sleeping form, "Nothing! I saved you. I now have you."

***

34

Dreamlife: There is the sound of wood on wood, bokken ricocheting off each other. The forearm numbing blows follow in blinding succession as the boys twist and twirl, side-step and lunge forward and always lush out, their wooden swords whistling through the mid-morning air.

Their adversary is the same age as they are. Dressed in the clothes of the sword-novice, as are they. They are all of the People.

He is not.

He falls back under the onslaught of the successive blows that descend on him. They push their advantage home, seeking to surround him. The boy they're fighting has round eyes. His straight black hair is cut short, same as theirs. The bokken whistle and hit wood, strike flesh. The boy's lips are pressed in a grim, thin line against the pain.

He doesn't cry out.

He takes their blows and fights back. They raise welts, on his shoulders and ribs and upper arms. Painful places, carefully chosen to hurt but not cripple. They don't want their quarry to give up too soon.

Sweat drips down all their faces. The round eyed boy is sporting a blood blister, as fat as a slug, hanging over his left eye, where the tempered wood brushed against his flesh but didn't break the skin.

He drops to one knee and scythes his bokken in a double-handed grip that slams against shins and grazes knees. Two of the boys go down, howling, and round-eyes springs up, his pain forgotten. With desperate energy he lays into the middle of them, keeping them busy, on the defensive, bunched in front of him. Were they to surround him he knows he's had it.

The pain from the blows he has taken however has taken its toll. A forward thrust catches him off guard, too slow to respond. The blunt end of a bokken strikes against his solar plexus, momentarily staggers him, sends him down to his knees. Immediately an older boy springs forward, his face a demon-mask of sweat and raw hate. He raises his own bokken high above his head with both hands and begins to bring it down on the unprotected head of the round eyed boy. A kiai, the scream of concentration begins to build up in his sternum. The blow of death.

"Kiyah!" there's a cry of surprise and the upraised bokken, struck out of the young boy's hand, goes sailing through the air. Like a whirlwind amongst them the large presence of Oku, the Retainer scatters the boys like chaff.

He lays into them with the scabbard of his long sword, placing his blows for maximum pain, minimum damage. They are his wards. He wants them unhurt but he'll be damned first before he suffers such insubordinate behaviour from any of them.

Howling and frightened now they scatter.

The round eyed boy looks up at the face of his saviour. The shaven dome of the forehead, the jet-black hair pulled back and tied in a bun. There is a glitter in the eyes of the Retainer that the boy has never seen there before.

"What is your name Ronin?" the Retainer addresses him in the tongue of the People and the boy answers in the same tongue.

"Rohan," he says and gets to his feet.

The Retainer throws back his big head with the long fencing scars down the side of one cheek and neck and he laughs. In the same motion he deals him a backhanded blow, sends him flat on his back.

"You fought well for a Ronin," he says "But you must learn respect for your betters."

With these words the Retainer walks away, his robes swishing with every move. The priests that have come with him make way respectfully, bow their heads in awe and he has a word with some of them.

There will be punishment met out tonight. Many boys will go to their pallets without any food and the gruelling hours spent in the training hall the following morning will seem that much longer to stomachs gnawed by hunger.

Rohan looks at the back of the Retainer and feels a mixture of pride and fear. His hunger the next day will be kept back by the will to do well. The Retainer's words: "You fought well," ring in his ears like bells of praise.

***

The next day the Slinger and Letitia set out early.

The night's slumber had worked its magic cure. Already there were healing scabs formed over most of the Slinger's wounds and some of the lesser ones had began to fade into bright pink welts that would vanish completely with time.

The Slinger took his freshly cleaned clothes, some dried meat and two water flasks, and paid the farmer with three silver coins. The man looked at the imperial dragon embossed on the metal and thanked him for his generosity.

The farmer's wife came to see them off. She gave them some vegetables, dried-up meat, bread, baked and preserved and told them where the next watering place could be found.

Letitia remained totally silent throughout.

"You have been kind to us," the Slinger said. He was eager to go, yet lingered on. There were still things he needed to know and the previous night's talk made him certain that here would be the clues he needed to find.

"Three days ago, there was a blond man on a pale charger, had eyes like yours," he told the woman and her husband looked up.

There were a few moments of silence before anyone spoke and then the farmer said: "Is the Law looking for him?"

"It's a question of kami, the gods of his ancestors. There's a blood-debt involved." the Slinger said and the farmer nodded in thought.

"He's a good man," he said, "the spring was drying, he made it flow again."

"How many days?"

"It is three, as you said, riding North."

The Slinger gave him one more silver coin, but the farmer refused to take it. "Only because it is kami," he said "He's a good man. Karma decides what will be."

The Slinger nodded in understanding and with Letitia in tow he rode off.

***

Dreamlife: "The first lesson is also the last." the Retainer says to them.

There are three hundred boys in the Training Hall, which is only a small part of the great Butokuden, Hall of the virtues of war.

They all stand in rows as he tells them they are useless, that less than half of them will survive the training to exchange their bokken for the great Katana, the long sword of the Slingers.

He speaks to them at length, waiting until the sweat has dried on their bodies and their muscles are cold and stiff and their brains dulled by talk. He then orders them to fall into groups of five. "Sixty battalions," he yells at them, "You're sixty battalions now you scum! To win a war you need to have spirit and strategy not numbers on your side." He's yelling at the top of his voice as he goes round, giving them orders, telling them what to do. "Numbers are for rats. So many rodent heads to blunt your stupid swords! Slingers win before the battle's even began and right now you're not much
better than rodents yourselves you worms!"

He breaks them up and goes round giving separate instructions and a password to each group. Some will be enemies, some will be friends, but no one will know who is what until they start fighting.

In Rohan's group there are four boys from the Nichiren Otto clan. They speak in whispers among themselves and decide that Rohan is to be liaison: expendable. His is the task to cross bokken first with each group and discover its allegiance. He is to take the blame for failure, should his own group fall to treachery.

Rohan bows to the older boy's command.

The training begins.

The entire Hall explodes into a whirling pattern of motion. Cries and yelps of pain and triumph mix with the groans of those hurt too badly to continue and the crack of thick wood on wood.

Rohan twists through the blurred motions of combat, exchanging passwords, finding those groups that share his own, guiding them towards the far left of the Hall where his own group is fighting, besieged by others.

Blood drips from skinned knuckles, where bokken have slipped along the length of his own and grazed him and his mind fights back animal signals of pain from a dozen strong blows. Determined, he runs and twists his body and speaks to those he is fighting, trying to sift through the enemies and find what allies he can.

He adds three groups to his own, sees his side strengthen its hold as the Nichiren clan boys give new orders, change their strategy so that they can fight in rotation, snatch a few precious moments of respite.

There is no such order for Rohan. He is sent out again. "Find more groups," they say, "We need more fighters."

He fights his way through increasingly hostile territory. More than once he gets to a group just as its defence pattern is broken and it is overwhelmed by those attacking.

He finds two more groups, bands them together. Sets them fighting in a double line, spin pattern. The longer arm of the water-wheel. It is daring strategy. If the centre doesn't hold they will be cut off. Those in the wings decimated.

They break through, join the others. They lose only one, in getting there.

Then there is the sound of the gong. The session is over.

Next to the Retainer strides a man dressed in Slinger black. He has the dragon star pinned to his chest and a fierce expression cast on his face. He has thrown his hood back and his head is exposed. The boys all kneel on the right knee as he surveys the carnage. Those that are not unconscious prostrate themselves in front of him.

"Who is he?" whispers Rohan and he is nudged from behind to be quite.

The man wears the two swords. The long one, strapped to his back, the shorter one worn at the waist. He steps over prostrate bodies and passes by the defeated groups, the boys' heads bowed in shame.

He stops in front of the group Rohan is in. As one the boys give him the bow of respect and submission. He still stands there.

"In the resolute acceptance of death," he says, addressing them in the High Speech of the People, Rohan struggles to understand, "there is no make believe. A bokken kills as well as a Katana."

He looks directly at Rohan. "Doubts in battle dissolve in the face of Happo Biraki."

He turns and strides out. The Retainer signals for the end of the session, the gong sounds twice and the boys begin helping up the injured, cleaning the blood off the floor. Bokken are put away.

Rohan ponders what has been said. Resolute acceptance of death. Happo Biraki: open on all eight sides. This is strategy he is unfamiliar with. One of the Nichiren Otto clan boys, the one Rohan knows as Oda, walks up to him.

"You did well," he says "it was an honour to be in your group."

Rohan looks startled. His group! It wasn't his group, he was just a part of it. It is the first time he's been shown friendliness by one of the People.

"Oda wait!" he says, eager to prolong the contact.

"Yes?" Other boys are staring openly now.

"Who was he? The man in black?"

"That was Musashi," Oda says, dropping his voice. "Imperial Slinger clan. He's the new Master."

"Thank you," Rohan says and finds that he can decipher the glances that are being cast his way. They are glances of shared pride. Pride they fought on the same side as he, and in some there is also a tinge of envy mixed with anger which he cannot decipher.

I must find out about Happo Biraki, Rohan thinks and bends to the task of cleaning the floor from the sweat and spilled blood, preparing the great Training Hall for the next session that will follow.

***

The sun rose and fell on them for two more days and nights and though the Slinger and Letitia rode due North the landscape did not change and there was no other sign of life.

The hard baked earth stretched as far as the eye could see bounded by barren hills that rose to hem in the horizon on three sides. What few plants braved the blazing sun and set root, were of a hardy variety, leathery green and short and they rooted in rocks and hollows, where the sun did not reach all the time.

In the first night they broke camp near some rocks. They sought shelter from the night's cold that came down from the star-studded sky.

The Slinger gathered some dry twigs, leafs and pieces of what looked like dried dung and lit a fire. There was little smoke from it but the smell was appalling.

"It'll keep the insects away," the Slinger explained making himself comfortable on one side of it. He'd wrapped himself up in his blanket, his two swords by his side and from a saddle bag he brought out the preserved bread the farmer's wife had so generously given them.

He broke that into small pieces, put half away and shared the rest with Letitia.

"It's funny to think there are so many lights," Letitia said. She was looking up at the sky.

The Slinger followed her gaze. He could see the constellations. The Swan and the Big Boar, the Executioner and further down, towards the east, the Face of Death, its fanged eye-teeth pointing their way.

"Worlds beyond compare," he said and Letitia looked startled.

"Worlds?"

"Like our own, it is said, but far, very far away. Where do you think I came from?"

"You were born, like all men."

"Uh-uh, round eyes have always come from the sky. Or their parents have, somehow the sky delivers round-eyes here. This world gives birth only to the People."

"You're...not one of the People but you're a Star-Slinger."

"I came from the sky."

Letitia shivered at that and wrapped her arms tightly about her. She watched the Slinger closely as he ate his bread, jaws moving methodically in the half-light of the fire.

Somewhere in the distance there was a lone howling and she started in fright.

"It's only a desert dog," the Slinger said, "they come out the moment it's dark."

She stood up to bring her blanket next to his and sat down, as close to him as she dared.

"Are we in danger?" she asked, but there was a calculating look in her eyes now. If the Slinger saw it he gave no indication. "No,"

She put a gentle hand on his leg, on the inside of his thigh, just above the knee. "Are your wounds still hurting?"

"The balm worked well, the harm is fading."

Her hand moved a little higher on his leg, squeezing gently, expertly.

"There were so many cuts, so much hurt..." she reached where she wanted.

He didn't try to stop her. But his body refused to react.

"It's so cold at night," there was a slight edge of pleading in her voice now, "too cold to sleep alone."

Something in what she'd said struck a resonant note in the Slinger. His hand picked up her own held it in front of the fire-light, but not before Letitia had felt his body finally give way. Begin at last to stir.

"I'm not what you think I am," he said to her.

"Please,"

"There is more to this than you see."

"Please," she was on her knees now, leaning above him, her lips nibbling at his chin, his lips, his temple.

There was no conflagration this time. No explosive release of pent-up uncontrolled emotion. His arms gently wrapped themselves round her body and he pulled her close.

His fingers moved over the fastenings of her clothes, released her body to the chill night air. He lingered over the goose bumps on her skin, his hands and lips explored what his eyes saw in the dancing firelight.

He spread his blanket for them both.

He was skilled. As skilled as he had been before. But he was different too this time. He was gentle in a way that no man had ever been with Letitia. He was considerate to the point that she suddenly felt touched, more respected and loved than at any other time in her life and the realisation brought glistening, unshed tears to her eyes.

The Slinger saw them and understood. He gently prized her legs apart, opened her to receive him. He held off for an instant, body poised above her like a sword.

Her hands played an intricate pattern on the muscled wall of his chest.

"Please," she whispered, "please." And he gave her the release she so eagerly sought. He lowered himself on top of her, losing himself in her reactions much as she lost herself in the uncontrolled emotions his lovemaking called up in her.

Later he held her in his arms as the sweat rapidly cooled their bodies.

"Thank you, thank you," she said in his ear her lips nibbling gently, kissing the soft earlobe.

The Slinger held her thus until sleep took them both.

In the morning they broke camp in silence and resumed their ride. The Slinger's thoughts were bent on the blond man riding ahead of them.

The blond man had left no more visible signs to mark his passage. He lit no fires, left behind no scraps of food and his horse seemed to choose the hardest parts of the earth to walk on.

The Slinger felt that the blond man was mocking him. He felt his life had entered a new phase at some stage and he was no longer in complete control but what that stage was or when it'd exactly happened he was not able to say.

"We are going to need more water." Letitia said to the Slinger's back.

Ever since they'd left the farmhouse he had taken to riding in front of her and she had accepted this as she had accepted everything else he did since she'd left with him from the nameless town near the desert. "The water flasks are almost empty."

The Slinger stopped his horse and waited for her to catch up. He sat tall in his saddle and pointed to the distant horizon, broken by the bare hills. "Over there should be the spring the woman spoke about," he said and resumed riding almost as if he felt guilty he'd spoken to her.

The place they reached was a clearing surrounded by sparse trees and strewn with rugged boulders. There was grass, fresh and green in this area and the Slinger dismounted and allowed the horses to graze. He scanned the area carefully, his eyes dark and inscrutable.

Letitia unsaddled the horses, unpacked one saddle bag and collected some dry wood from around the roots of the trees. Rubbing two sticks together, she painstakingly got a small fire going. She took out a can and poured in the last of the water and the few remaining vegetables they had taken with them. After that they would have to rely on dried meat and hard baked bread and whatever the Slinger could kill, to survive.

Throughout this work the Slinger remained immobile crouched on the ground in the middle of the clearing, away from the fire. He could sense a threat in this place but he could not put his finger on it. He unsheathed his long sword and held it in front of him and his eyes scanned everything but there was nothing to see.

Presently he stood up and strode up to the fire and the soup Letitia was preparing. He took the helping she offered him and sat down to think about the subtle hints of danger he felt emanating all around.

The horses were unaffected by it, grazing peacefully, so it was probably aimed only at humans. He looked up at the sky that was slowly darkening and decided it was too late to look for another place to spend the night.

"Do not get out of sight in this area," he said to Letitia and she looked up sharply at him.

"Why?"

"The blond man's been here, I can feel it," he said, but he couldn't and it puzzled him.

Letitia brought her hand out of her pocket and there clutched in her fist was one of the bluestone amulets he'd seen the residents of the nameless town wear.

"Is it safe?"

"There is no immediate danger."

Letitia absorbed the information and nodded quietly. After they'd finished their simple meal she got up to fetch some water.

The farmer's wife had spoken truthfully and there was a fresh water spring bubbling from between the rocks at one side of the clearing. The water was cold and it tasted faintly of metal from the bowels of the earth.

When Letitia came back the Slinger was whetting the shorter of the two swords he carried, his lips made the same eerie sound as he drew the silk was across the gleaming edge of the blade and she took a deep breath to relieve the superstitious awe this sound inspired. Despite his extraordinary killing abilities the Slinger was only flesh and blood she reminded herself. She stole a quick look at him, but he was totally ignoring her.

She debated whether it would be worth making him notice her again, forcing herself to his attention. Her eyes took on a dreamy expression as she remembered the effect she had had on him the night before. He seemed to have regretted his taking her and he had spent all day in moody withdrawal.

Darkness came rapidly in these parts she thought and the riding made her feel tired. She didn't quite understand the Slinger's obsession with the blond man since it was not a matter of Law but she wasn't complaining. Her dreary existence in the nameless town by the desert had receded into a sort of dream-like past and the memory of the denigrations she'd suffered there had already began to fade.

Taking her blanket she brought it as close to the fire as she could, wrapped herself up in it and was soon sound asleep.

On the other side of the fire, like an ebony sentinel, the Slinger continued to clean and croon to his weapons, waiting for his senses to tell him that it was safe enough to go to sleep.

He'd been trained to allow his mind to float, to seek the No-mind condition that in Zen stood for ultimate knowledge. The threat he sensed round him grated on his ability to feel the insubstantial, but there was nothing he could focus on. It was like a smouldering anger waiting, just out of reach. Waiting for the appropriate trigger that would set it off.

After the moon had set, he put his sword beside him and stretched out next to the fire to doze.

***

The wailing cries of the woman woke him. His consciousness stirred slowly from the depths of a slumber that was not of his own making and he struggled to come to the surface.

Letitia was cavorting, wrapped in her blankets on the other side of the dying embers of the fire. Her eyes were tightly shut against the night and she had bunched her hands into fists and drawn them close to her chest and her legs were curled up in her stomach.

"Letitia!" the Slinger called out her name and tried to restrain her but she was lost in whatever force now gripped her and continued wailing and cavorting.

A sudden wind rose and stirred the tops of the trees circling the clearing and Letitia's wailing seemed to be echoed by the darkness all around. The Slinger lifted his hand and slapped her hard, once, twice, sent her head reeling from side to side and Letitia's eyes snapped open.

They were the eyes of a corpse, cold and unseeing and the Slinger drew out a thin sliver of steel, reflecting the cold starlight and whatever light the dying embers still had inside them and he moved the blade before her eyes, playing it over his fingers so that it seemed to come to life and snake across the outside of his open hand.

Letitia's wailing stopped and her eyes followed the path of the shiny blade and then, suddenly, they were filled with the light of recognition and there was an instant of horror drawn deep in them, before they unfocused completely and slowly rolled behind her head. Her body stopped its cavorting and slumped in the Slinger's arms.

The wailing now was all around them and the Slinger realised the nature of the threat.

He quickly searched the woman's clothes and found the bluestone amulet she had pulled out earlier and put it around her neck. The bluestone shone eerily in the starlight and he hoped that for now it would hold her, keep her safe from harm.

The wind picked up speed and the tree-tops whipped in a frenzy and the unearthly wailing rose even higher and the Slinger stood up and dropped his two swords by the fire, beside the place he had slept.

He thought he should have seen it earlier, realised what was happening but his thoughts had been trailing after the blond man on the pale charger and since the desert crossing he had been slow in his thinking and slow to act.

This was the only watering place for a large area, the spring flowed despite the aridity that held the land in its grip and travellers, in these parts, were mainly male.

He stepped away from the clearing towards the rocks where the clear water flowed and the spirit of the spring called out to him. A coalesced glowing form, that gained solidity, floated over the water.

A naked woman, fulsome, fertile, with large, round breasts and the flaring hips of a breeder, beckoned to him and he felt his body betray him once more, the surge of unbridled lust coursed through him and, against all reason, he wanted her.

Wanted her badly.

Ignoring the demands made by his tumescent flesh, he dropped to his knees, his fingers knotted themselves in the intricate pattern of his clan's prayer, *Heaven and Earth, Fire and Water*. He closed his eyes and concentrated seeking to get to the centre of her. The power that lived in the spring.

Against his shut eyelids he saw the image of the woman dissolve, the true serpentine form of the lamia take its place, the mouth wailing and as the female eyes shed their tears of impassioned anguish he heard her voice.

"*Give. Give a little.*"

"No!" he resisted. His lust was gone and he now felt nothing for her, his compassion had dried long ago.

"*You must give. You must give a little. You're a Star-Slinger. You burn so bright.*" and she writhed and twisted, the serpentine rings uncoiling and she shed human tears from her eyes.

He would not be thwarted. "Leave the woman alone," he commanded.

"*Give, just a little.*"

"No."

"*A bargain. Then let us bargain.*" the lamia entreated and the Slinger felt the surging presence of her, hovering expectantly all around and against the back of his shut eyelids he saw what she was pointing at and realised then the true nature of the trap the blond man had left for him at the nameless town by the desert.

He saw the future blacken, narrow to a single thread, as all paths he had taken, every decision he'd made, all stopped at the town. All, save the thread he was looking at now: him and Letitia riding out of the town together. He knew what it meant. *Kami*, he thought, a blood bond. The blond man had left him no alternative, Letitia had truly saved his life. Kami now bounded her to him and he knew the compromise that meant to the power of his purpose. He threw his head back and howled then. A howling that matched and surpassed the lamia's wailing and she shrank back, in fear of his anger and the wind dropped a notch.

"*A bargain,*" she pleaded "*we both stand to gain.*" And he knew what she was asking of him and, unwillingly, he slowly dropped his defences, and gave in to her demands.

Immediately there was the pressure of female on him, in him, in parts of him that nothing had ever touched and as she drunk of those parts of him that his training had taught him to shape, where anger and lust and pain and pleasure and the inborn love for death deeply dwelled, she revealed the future to him. She let him see the blond man riding ahead and a place of doom deep in the bowels of the earth and Letitia drowning beneath murky waves.

"No!" he cried. Was he doomed to bring death to everyone he met?

"*A bargain's a bargain, I can't change what you saw.*"

"Is there no hope then?"

"*Hope? You ask of hope? There's the blood of innocents staining your blade. You carry the burden of guilt on your soul. What need you hope?*"

"I must know," he insisted.

"*You'll catch him. He goes North, to his place of power.*"

"I can defeat him. I can!" He yelled out at her but she was gone. He felt the wrenching of her leaving, the draining of energy that was part of his life and he did not begrudge her that, for at the same time he felt the depths of the soul that guided her and it was ruled by loneliness. A loneliness so deep and so unrelieved as to remain as pure as the No-mind his masters had attained, the void of Zen Musashi had taught him to seek in battle, the state of grace where all things dissolved into nothingness, and the lamia had it, was afflicted with it. Lived because of it.

The wind died down. There was quiet. His thigh muscles trembling with exhaustion the Slinger went back to his blanket by the now dead fire.

Letitia was sleeping soundly, her face completely at rest. The Slinger pulled out his two swords and put them down beside him. He wrapped himself up in his blanket and stole one last look at the woman. The realisation of the burden she'd placed on him made him see her in a new light. He had a brief replay of the vision of waves engulfing her again and he forcefully pushed it out of his mind.

This was not going to happen.

There was a sensation of peace and gratitude emanating from the clearing. The Slinger closed his eyes and slept quietly and despite his fatigue and exhaustion, this time he slept lightly, as he'd been trained to do and his consciousness remained aware of every blade of grass and tree leaf that rustled in the breath of the morning breeze, so that when sunlight first broke in the sky, Letitia woke to find him stoking the fire, some dried meat already warming on it.

Unaware of what had happened during the night she smiled sweetly at him and this time, to her delighted surprise, the Slinger smiled back.

Chapter 3

The Oracle

The visions the lamia had shown the Slinger, her inhuman touch and the familiar taste of loneliness he had felt was her soul, they combined with the burden of guilt he carried with him to drive a wedge of despair deep in him.

The lamia had been right of course. There was the blood of innocents staining his sword. He carried that burden along with so others on his soul.

Had he managed to fight off the inertia of *gaffla* when he should, he'd never have lingered in the nameless town long enough for the blond man's spell to work. "He may know me better than I know myself," he whispered to himself and Letitia who was riding a few feet behind him thought he had spoken to her.

Out of the corner of his eye he saw something dancing in the distant horizon that gave him some hope.

"What did you say?"

He turned his attention to her, studying her face for signs of the previous night's struggle. Her dark eyes remained as clear as the midday sky.

"We must break off and go east for a while." he said.

"Why?"

He waited until she was next to him and then pointed at the barely visible simmering outline of a rock in the distance. It rose towards the sky above like a sorcerer's wand, gnarled and twisted.

In the morning heat-haze it seemed to dance.

"A retreat," he said, "there must be an oracle nearby,"

"There are no oracles in these parts, there haven't been for a long time."

"You can't be sure of that."

"If there were the men of the town would have known and they would have come here."

The Slinger made an impatient move with his gloved hand, "We must make sure there isn't one. A chance like this may not come again where we're going and it's important," he said and set off at a fast trot.

Letitia was left to follow behind as best as she could.

As he rode he thought of the blond man now unexpectedly putting more ground between them and he ran his personal mantra through his mind again: I can defeat him, I can defeat him, I can defeat him.

He was conscious of the fact that this little detour gave perhaps the opportunity to the blond man to escape.

But if there was an oracle. If the twisted rock that marked the retreat, housed indeed a Lady with the Sight, perhaps a certain way could be found to thwart the outcome of the visions the lamia had given him.

The Slinger owed it to himself to at least try.

As they rode nearer the rock became clearer and clearer.

It rose indeed like a pretzel, all twisted and gnarled, its top spiralling up at the sky, crumbling already from the combined effects of wind, rain and sun to a wicked looking point, like a witch's overgrown nail.

At its feet were the customary caves. Their openings cleverly disguised with shrubs.

"It's so quiet here." Letitia said.

They'd stopped trotting now and the horses seemed to slow down without needing to be told.

Despite the heat of the sun overhead there was a certain

preternatural chill to the air. The rays of the sun hit the rock at an angle so that it threw a long shadow.

Letitia rubbed her upper arms with her hands, "I don't like this place," she said.

They stood in front of the half-hidden openings of the caves, waiting.

The Slinger said nothing.

He could feel the power emanating in the air and he motioned for Letitia to stop.

"We come without fear," he said.

His words were thrown back at him, like a slap, by the rock.

"We come without anger," he said.

They waited for some response and when none was forthcoming the Slinger handed the reins of his horse to Letitia and dismounted slowly.

Fresh from his experience with the lamia he felt attuned to the feel of magic and the hair at the nape of his neck stood up on end as he neared the rock.

"We seek your guidance."

The Slinger's voice this time was a lot more quiet. Within the deep shadows of the caves he'd seen some movement.

The sense of emanating power intensified all around them. One of the horses let out a snort and shook its head up and down and Letitia had to pull sharply on the reins to quieten it.

"You may come in Slinger." the voice startled them both.

Letitia had to struggle to stifle a scream from escaping. One of the horses reared up, front hoofs flailed at the empty air and the Slinger had to make a visible effort to stop his sword-arm from reaching for his Katana.

The palpable emanations around them were now tinged with danger.

"We mean you no harm." the Slinger said, edging closer.

"I know," again the same startlingly powerful voice, neither male nor female coming as if from the very depths of the rock itself.

"You may come in, but the woman must remain where she is."

The Slinger turned towards Letitia and she nodded.

Turning back to the entrances to the caves the Slinger bent low and passed into the first one. Immediately he was transported into a cool, dark world of smells of rotting flesh and half-shadows.

The emanations of power he'd felt outside were so much stronger here, tinged with what?

Fear? Danger?

He wasn't at all sure now.

"I have come to seek guidance."

"Guidance yes. Such an easy word," the voice boomed again.

It was a strange choice of words made even stranger by the fact that it marked behaviour the Slinger knew well no true Oracle would display.

"I have left the woman outside. Will you not reveal yourself to me now?" he asked.

"You're a Star-Slinger." the voice said.

"You can see that."

"Yet you're not of the People."

"I'm a Star-Slinger," the Slinger said, "this alone is sufficient,"

He cast his gaze around the cave. There were garments of several different designs strewn on stools and over the floor. Wooden boxes of different sizes piled on top of one another and against one corner, forming almost the perfect place for someone to hide behind.

There was no light in the cave, and by the smell of it the Slinger could tell that it had not been cleaned for a long time.

"Hold your sword Star-Slinger." the powerful, androgynous voice said, "I'm coming out to see you."

Indeed there was some motion at the back of the cave, where the boxes had been piled high and a young boy appeared, not much taller than four foot.

It moved slowly, timidly, as if afraid the Slinger would pounce upon it. It was dressed in what appeared to be rags, home-made clothes cobbled together from dresses and its feet were bare.

But it was the eyes that drew and retained the Slinger's attention. The eyes of the boy were devoid of youth. There was an old soul looking out from the depths of those eyes.Their look told him all he wanted to know.

They were in no immediate danger.

"You're not the oracle." he said he felt strangely defeated. He had wasted precious time to get here.

"The Oracle died a long time ago, I only preserve the shadow of the spirit she was," said the young boy with the age-old eyes.

As it spoke, the Slinger noticed, it did not move its lips, yet the voice was still as powerful as before.

"You can only hear me in your head," the boy explained.

The Slinger felt a brief rekindling of hope.

"Can you help me?" he asked.

Surely if the boy had such powers, it was conceivable it might have others.

"You're beyond my help Slinger." it said, "You've already fought and won all your battles and you have losses to suffer in the time ahead, I'm no Oracle to foretell the future."

The Slinger took one step towards it, "But you can surely see."

"I can see the mark of the lamia upon you. That I can see plain as day. But the future? That is closed to me."

"How did the Oracle die?"

"She died alone," the boy said.

The Slinger felt the first stirrings of anger inside him, he was not to be trifled with by a child.

"She died in trance!" the boy said quickly.

Apparently it could read the Slinger's thoughts, or at the very least his intentions.

"I was the acolyte here. But I was brought here far too young and, as it turned out, far too late. The Oracle was too old even as I came to be taught. When she died, all she could do was pass some of her spirit to me. Now the future is locked away from me forever."

"So, there is no hope," the Slinger made to leave.

"Wait!"

He turned back.

"The future may be closed, but I can see what you are. Now."

"I hear you."

The child took on a solemn expression. The wizened eyes became suddenly fixed and the voice inside the head of the Slinger took on strong female overtones.

"I see the lamia has changed you. Death himself has touched you...and changed you. You're the avenger of the sum of your deeds and

54

you seek an adversary. A blond man on a powerful steed, but you need look for him no further than you need. The adversary you seek is already within you."

There was silence. The Slinger waited for a few moments longer but the child did not move. Its old eyes were shut now. Its body held rigid.

How much could he trust a half-Reading by an inexperienced acolyte? Even one as gifted as this young boy was? How much of the true oracle's spirit did the boy possess?

If the boy heard his mental questioning it chose not to allay any of the Slinger's misgivings.

"Thank you," the Slinger said, seeing nothing more would be forthcoming.

The boy's eyelids fluttered and snapped open.

"Did you get what you wanted?"

It was the hope in the voice that made the Slinger feel sick inside. So much was being lost. So much had been lost already. This was just another line in an endless litany of losses.

"Yes," he said and brought his hand to his chest, to cover the silver star with its dragon. "I found your words of immeasurable help."

He was careful to keep his private thoughts artfully hidden. The boy's face seemed to instantly brighten.

"Your woman perhaps would like a Reading then too?"

"We have tarried too long already," the Slinger said, bowing formally, "there's a long distance to cover and we must ride hard."

"Oh," the boy looked disappointed, "you'll be back this way perhaps?"

"That we will." the Slinger said and saw the shy smile come back on, "Meantime we'll tell all we pass of the Oracle's words. It is fitting that greater tribute is paid to you here."

"Go with my blessing then Slinger," the boy said ritually. It sounded incongruous coming from the lips of one so young, and in its happiness the boy had forgotten itself.

Its voice was thin and reedy and childish, not yet broken by age and experience.

The Slinger bowed one more time and retreated.

Once outside he took the reins of his horse from Letitia and leapt on the waiting steed's broad back.

"Well?" she looked at him enquiringly and all he could see was the vision the lamia had given him.

The one that mustn't pass!

"Let's go!" he yelled to her turning his horse and spurring the beast into a gallop, "The blond man's ahead of us and we've a lot of ground to cover!"

Chapter 4

The Shining Star

*D*reamlife: "Run Rohan, run! Do you want to be left behind?"

Their cries are drowned in laughter as they race each other through the tall bamboo grass and the prairie wind, coming down from the mountains, ruffles their hair and brings down Spring smells that fire their blood.

It is growing longer now, as they progress through the ranks of the sword-novice.

Their skill with the bokken is increasing along with their knowledge of strategy. Oku, the Retainer, never stops making fun of them and their attempts to fold their hair up in a bun, like his.

"Oda, wait!" Rohan calls out and they all stop running and wait.

Ever since that day in the Great Hall, when the Great Master signalled him out and spoke to him, his life has taken a turn for the better.

The People accept him as one of their own and no longer taunt him and say he dropped from the sky like bird-dropping. His round eyes still draw attention in the Great Hall but the People are more used to them now and he is grateful that they're the midnight black of the People, rather than the usual sky-blue of the emperor's cats.

"What is it?"

"Over there. By the trees, I thought I saw something move." Rohan points to the clump of trees where he's seen the flash of movement and the boys stretch to their full height to look over the tall grass.

"Let's go take a look," Oda suggests and the others, Oki, and Udu and Yohito readily ascent their heads nodding in unison as the light of mischievous glee and adventure lights their faces.

Rohan hesitates. They are his escort, the ones he has chosen to accompany him to the City, where his father, back from spending his days with the emperor's entourage, waits to meet him. They have been granted only four days.

Four days of freedom, without the shadowy presence of the Master and the overbearing Oku to tell them what worms they are and how he will crash them beneath the heel of his boot. Wearing their bokken, in open country, they are kings, the High Road open to them day and night. No peasant would dare challenge their right to travel on it, or anywhere else they want for that matter.

"Come on Rohan!"

"All right," he says "but we mustn't dally long." They have silver in their pockets, large round coins with the red dragon of the Imperial Mint and Oda has promised to take them all to the brothels. The red-lanterned sin-palaces he's heard the Slinger warriors visit on their return from a battle. He has regaled them all with visions of exotic concubines skilled in singing and dancing and the telling of long tales. He's described to them time and again, in great detail, how these concubines have skins smooth as ivory and luminous slanted eyes and they're trained from birth in the pleasuring of a man's body and they have listened avidly, their new-found lust boiling just beneath the surface of their young, taut bodies.

Which explains why they are travelling through the open fields, so far off the emperor's High Road that leads directly to the City.

They crawl on their bellies through the tall grass and reach a small rise where some hedges that have taken root will hide them from view. They part the branches slowly, careful not to disturb the hedges more than the motion of the slight breeze would warrant, and stare aghast.

There is a man and a woman coupling furiously on the forest floor. The man is a Retainer, his open robe and shed jacket carry the markings of the House of Hishito, the same Imperial red dragon that they carry on the coins that weigh down their pockets is boldly embossed on the leather of his black saddle.

It must have been the man riding in by the trees, that Rohan saw out of the corner of his eye. There is an algae filled lake directly in front of them and the couple.

Behind the furiously coupling pair the forest stretches as far as the eye can see. A small winding path skirts the length of the lake and comes to the clearing, the road the horseman probably took to get there. Parts of the road are exposed to a view from the fields.

The woman is dressed in the clothes of a royal concubine. They can not make out the markings for her kimono is open and the man is covering her body with his own, his bare buttocks pistoning up and down between her parted legs.

They are both making choked, urgent sounds.

The boys watch speechlessly. When the couple have finished they both stand up and quickly rearrange their clothes. The woman's kimono is marked with a red rose. None of them has seen that marking before.

They are too far away to hear what the man and woman are saying to each other clearly, but the lake is very narrow where they are and the wind blowing through the gap between the low hills and the trees picks up snippets of conversation and brings it, floating, down to them.

"...everything as ordered," the woman says and the next gust brings part of the man's answer to them.

"...women and children will be slaughtered."

The woman averts her face at this and says something they cannot hear and then the man is speaking again: "Better that than to live by the sword. We must let the children go to the lamb..."

"Everyone?"

"...two days gone."

And then the man gets on his horse and rides off and the woman looks around suspiciously before she too disappears back into the forest, taking a narrow path between the trees that is almost invisible from where they are.

"What do you make of that?" Oda asks thoughtfully.

"Beautiful woman," Rohan replies and Uku punches him playfully on the shoulder, licks his lips lewdly and giggles. Yoshito giggles too, only Oda remains serious.

Oda whose father is in the Imperial secret police and has often heard talk of intrigue.

"What do you think?" Rohan asks him sensing his seriousness.

"They are spies, or worse."

"Do you think we should tell?"

"We must! It's our duty to the emperor!"

Rohan thinks about it. "How shall we explain our presence here?"

"We were tired. We were looking for a lake to drink some water from, so we left the High Road and found ourselves here." Uku says and they all look at each other.

"Nothing else." Rohan admonishes them.

"Nothing else." They all agree.

***

"Your Retainer tells me you're doing well." says his father's concubine and Rohan looks down in respect.

"Yes," he says, not meeting her eye. The woman is beautiful, young, younger than his father and she is clearly more than a mere concubine. Her stately elegance and grace speak of zaibatsu, old family money. The last of a line that has produced no males, or else war has claimed them all.

Her name is Yukio and she has chosen to stay with his father. Rohan knows well the sacrifice of a choice such as this. His father is a round-eyes, like himself. The man of the gun. The only one in all the empire to carry such a weapon. People say that he has dropped from the sky. For Yukio to live with him it means the end of an honourable line. No round eyed man can inherit the name and power of a family of the People.

60

"You are also very troubled," she says "is it because of what you've told your father?"

Rohan doesn't answer her. She is not his mother, she has no claim on him. He knows it is her money that pays for him at the Great Hall and he resents it.

"Why does my father not marry you?" he asks suddenly and instantly regrets the impulse. His father, once angered, is quite capable of taking the scourge to him, whipping the flesh from his bones.

Yukio, sits back, on her haunches and looks at him. She reaches out between them and takes one of the elaborately ornamented tea cups that have been layed out by the servants. She drinks deeply from it, puts it down and then goes through the entire elaborate process of pouring more tea for them both.

"Your father serves the emperor," she says looking at him carefully, studying the signs that tell her that he knows well what she's doing, "As you will one day. It serves the emperor better to have your father unmarried."

Before Rohan can reach for the elaborately poured tea cup she dismisses him.

Rohan does not understand, will not understand until it is too late. He will then admire the deep resolve of his father, the elegance of the woman he loved but chose not to marry for reasons of politics. He will then realise, slowly, like dew sipping through a crack in the rocks until a pool forms, that they and those they served were, even then, pitting their passion and lives against the welling of the darkness around them and it wasn't enough.

Not nearly enough.

In the end it had seen them come undone. The blond man had seen to it. The House of the Rose, of which he knew nothing at the time, and those others that had listened to what the blond man preached.

His father listened carefully to Rohan's account and the boys' description of the events in the forest and then he'd left to see the emperor. "There'll be a purge over this," he'd muttered his handsome face darkening, "the last thing we need."

And that night Rohan had been left in the house alone with Yukio, the concubine, who'd ceremoniously poured him tea but hadn't let him drink it.

In the dark of the night the blond man had come riding with six servants, all armed to the teeth.

"Message from the Emperor! Message from the Emperor!" he'd yelled not waiting to be invited in, but pushing his way past the sole protesting house-keeper.

He'd spent a long time that night alone with Yukio and when he'd left again, just before daybreak, waking his riders with more yells and shouts Rohan had heard Yukio cry, but he hadn't understood.

Not then.

***

At noon, they stopped their hard ride to give the tired horses a break and the Slinger found a warren hidden amongst the base of the trees and he waited. When he spied a movement through the rocks and underbrush his hand flicked out, a thin blade whistled through the air and he killed the rabbit before it could get back into its hole.

He carefully skinned it and roasted it over a fire and he smoked that part of the meat they were not going to eat to last a few more days.

Letitia watched all this with interest, pondering the change she could see in him. He was still sullen and quiet but a lot more responsive to her. He acknowledged her presence and answered her questions.

"What has he done? This blond man you're chasing?" she asked as they ate and he stopped chewing his meat and looked up. He had tied his long black hair back with a black ribbon and he looked more handsome than ever.

"He killed my father," he said and resumed chewing on the rabbit.

"I heard people talk about him," she said "the man with hair the colour of gold and the eyes of a cat. I never thought I'd meet him. He's a sorcerer isn't he?"

"Maybe, maybe not."

"Can he do anything to hurt you?"

The Slinger didn't answer her. He finished his meal and drunk some water and then took out the folded leather map from one of his pockets. He spread it out on a rock, near the fire and looked at the path they had taken.

The map was sketchily marked, large patches of territory were uncharted blanks. And now they will never be charted, he thought, for those who would have done the charting are gone, replaced by the rabble.

He thought of Disruption and for the first time since they'd left the farmhouse allowed his mind to return to the words of the oracle the Lady of the Reading had given him.

A lot had happened between his coming out of the desert and now, and he had a blood bond on him. His instincts told him that the blond man was slowing, that the distance was closing. He was probably no more than two days ahead now. Ever heading due North, towards the mountains. What did he hope to find there? What manner of strength would he gain? He thought.

With a gloved finger he traced the path the blond man was taking. It went through blank areas of map and crossed over the mountains. The mountains were marked with crosses. The sign of mines. The lamia had spoken of a place of doom, deep in the earth, but the Slinger knew about the lines of possibility and the fluxity of *Karma*. The lamia could only read what would happen from the here and now. The future born of the future was beyond her reach, its Time removed from her.

The Slinger looked at the angle of the sun, calculating the hours of hard riding they had left.

"Let's go," he said to Letitia and she, content to just be with him, stifled the stiffness and fatigue of the ride and the sleepiness of food at midday and hastened to obey.

***

"Those who yield do not need to bother wearing a sword," Oku strikes out with every word, the thrusts and sweeps of his bokken drive them back steadily.

He is stripped to the waist, the great glistening bulk of his oiled body, dripping with sweat, the shaved dome of his head shining.

Armed with the lighter shinai, the pliable bamboo sword of the sword-novice, Rohan and Oda fall back. Rohan signals to Oda, to feign to the right, to force the Retainer to expose his flank. Oda moves as fast as he can.

Fails.

"Kiyah dogspawns! You'll have to do better than that!" the Retainer counters Oda's thrust making him lose his balance and stumble between Rohan and him. Cursing Rohan has to fall further back, nearer the blazing coal pit whose ferocious heat he can feel singe his back. The Retainer laughs louder.

Rohan lashes out harder, his bamboo sword a blur. The Retainer bears down upon them now, drawn by their defensive attitude, the course of last resort, he strikes their weapons aside contemptuously, deals them blows to arms and legs, the thick wooden tip of the bokken, causing them blinding pain that momentarily paralyses their limbs.

"Kiyah! Dogs! Today you burn!" he pushes them relentlessly back, past the safe distance mark. Rohan feels the heat of the coals rise from the pit and soak through their thin clothing. He chances a look back and sees the yawning mouth of it barely three paces beyond their heels.

"Yield!" the Retainer shouts.

Rohan looks sideways at Oda. Oda has taken a blow to the temple, his eyes are glazing and he is gritting his teeth against the pain and the rolling waves of unconsciousness, fighting to stay on his feet. Thick droplets of sweat mixed with blood roll down his face to stain the collar of his tunic.

"Yield!"

"Never!" Rohan shouts back and thrusts the tip of his bamboo sword at the Retainer's face hoping to catch him in a blink, immediately changes direction, rotating his bamboo sword to strike low, on the outside of the knee joint, where he knows it'll hurt, but Oku is a war veteran. He has survived battles where ten thousand a side were lost.

He shows Rohan his teeth in a big smile and almost gently pushes Oda's bamboo sword aside and taps him in the centre of the chest.

Oda overbalances, his knees crumble and he starts to fall towards the pit. With a yell Rohan turns his body sideways, closing the outside points of attack. He throws his bamboo sword at Oku's face and as the Retainer ducks Rohan grabs Oda's falling body and pushes him sideways, away from the lip of the yawning pit and the burning coals. Oda falls on his side and lies unmoving.

"Yield!" the Retainer says and Rohan now smiles, teeth bared in a feral, desperate grin. At the edge of his vision he sees a shadow move on the battlements, behind the silent forms of the boys that watch their session with Oku. He turns to face the Retainer.

"Never," he says quietly and hears the moan of regret from the boys as within full sight of the silent form of Musashi, who stands watching, arms folded across his chest, Rohan stands and accepts the blow that knocks him unconscious.

***

He walks through the passages of the emperor's Keep unchallenged. His round eyes tell the guards instantly who he is.

The Keep walls are thick and in places wet with damp. There is a mustiness to the entire place. A feeling of suffocation, like clouds have descended to the earth and breathing is now a problem. The walls, as he passes them speak to him of age, of time, of valorous deeds performed here, but he's in a hurry.

He reaches the prison cells. The long double row of iron-shod doors, each with an iron grill in the centre looks intimidating. "Oda," he calls out and his friend's face appears at one of openings.

"Rohan!" Oda yells, he sounds all surprised. "What are you doing here?"

Rohan walks up to him, his friend's face through the grill looks puffy and swollen.

One eye is shut.

"Came to see you," he says, "Oku is missing you. His stick's getting idle without your thick head around."

Oda grins. "I'll be out soon."

"How did it happen?"

"I don't know Rohan. I don't know. I was down in the brothels. They gave me sake to drink, I was too drunk to remember much. I think some men broke in, when I was with the women-"

"They say you killed three Imperial guards. Oku's privately thrilled. He says he always thought the guards were prostitutes in their free time, now he's convinced."

Oda lets out a laugh. "Don't hit him too hard until I get out."

"He told me to tell you he's waiting."

"Good. Good. Train hard, Rohan."

They clasp hands through the narrow bars of the grill.

"See you soon."

Rohan's steps take him back through the labyrinthine passages, past guards who know him, past doors housing prisoners of every description, past rooms from which the sound of guards revelling escapes, past armouries and swordsmiths immersed in the heat of forging new metal and past the kitchens, situated below mid-level where the cooks now labour and mouth-watering smells waft out.

He heads towards the top part of the Keep, where strategies are layed out and his father spells out his elaborate plans to the emperor's military staff.

Going past a Keep window that overlooks a tiny courtyard, surrounded by high walls, Rohan's eyes catch a scene he'll remember forever.

There are two men in the courtyard, dressed in Slinger black, Imperial guards line one side. Against the far wall kneeling in the dirt, are four men and a woman with their hands tied behind their back.

Rohan recognizes one of the men and the woman. They are the couple he and the others observed in the forest. The woman has her head bent, sobbing fitfully. The other three men are silent. The woman's lover does not bow his head in submission when the Slingers approach him. He spits at them.

The woman lifts her tear-streaked face at this, looks at the Slingers. "You'll all burn for this," she cries, "You will burn!"

Unmoved, untouchable, the Slingers unsheathe their swords. Rohan doesn't want to watch. He's seen beheadings before. This time however, it's a little different, this time he has been, however indirectly, involved, and he's unable to tear his eyes away.

"A visitor to the Keep?"

Rohan turns to see who is addressing him. The words are in the tongue of the round eyes and Rohan who has not spoken it for most of his life has to think hard before he understands what has been said.

The man who has spoken is tall and slim, with long blond hair and a beard and the deep blue eyes of the Emperor's cats. He is dressed in leathers of brown and wears a shirt of pure white and boots that match the colour of his leather trousers and he has no weapon. Red wings have been stitched on the leather at his breast. The jacket, Rohan notices, has metal teeth on the trim, just like his father's.

"Who are you?" Rohan challenges him in the speech of the People, putting his hand on his bokken.

The stranger smiles unconcerned. "More to the point, who are you? And what are you doing here little round eyes?"

"I am here to see Oda Nuhura, of the Nichiten Otto clan. Who are you round eyes?"

Rohan returns the insult and the blond man lets his smile broaden further.

"I'm the Emperor's seer," says the man and his eyes widen so that for a moment Rohan thinks he can see dark shadows swimming in the blue behind them, "I foretell what is to come,"

Rohan sneers. In the Great Hall he's been taught to hold respect for the Ladies of the Reading, the Keepers of The Book. He knows that there are others who claim to share in this ability to see the future, Oku calls them charlatans, frauds.

"Tell then seer," Rohan challenges.

"And be damned?" the blond man sneers.

"You need your crystal bauble perhaps?"

"Careful round eyes, you may displease me and then the future shall darken for you and there'll be no little shining star to lead the children forth in their hour of need."

"What?"

"All men need a leader. The moment chooses who leads more than the slant of their eyes, my little sword-novice. Those who follow the Way should never forget that."

And the blond man is gone leaving Rohan in a sudden whirl of confusion.

In the window below him, the execution has already taken place and the Imperial guards are busy hauling the beheaded bodies away.

***

The blond man had said just that: the shining star, and the Slinger

67

was not yet sure what he had meant by that.

In the years that followed the Star-Slingers had blazed forth displaying valour the like of which the world was never to see again. A bright star had flared up in the sky. It was the star that led to the discovery of the baby whose death roused the peasants. It set in motion the events that eventually killed his father.

The blond man had betrayed them all, when they needed him the most.

The Slinger looked at Letitia, the straight black hair and slight, almost delicate physique, the smooth brown skin. His thoughts tagged back to the day of the riding, when Rie had stood at the window of the Emperor's Keep and waved goodbye while he and Oda and Uku and the others rode out to join the emperor, riding ahead with his father, secure in their foolish dreams of victory.

Unaware that the battle had been lost before it had even began.

When they understood, it was too late. The day of steel, and sorrow had come. The day when the long swords had flashed in the sun and the streets had run red with blood, to no avail.

The false pyre of righteousness had taken hold of the crowd and the Keep had been lost.

Rie had burnt at the stake and the Slinger had watched it. Her body had twisted and blackened and to the last, she had died crying out his name.

The Slinger motioned to Letitia to ride beside him and she spurred her horse to trot faster. He thought about this strange woman who had placed such an unwanted burden on him. The lamia had seen it and had used her to get to him. He thought that it would perhaps be wiser to learn something of her. A way perhaps could be found to ease his debt to her, lessen the bond.

Kami, he thought, the blood of the ancestors. Who would have ended his life had Letitia not saved him?

He looked at the sun to calculate the remaining hours.

"We'll stop in a while," he said, "rest some and ride through the night. We are getting nearer."

Letitia nodded her head in agreement. He never used to consult her before, or even tell her anything. She found herself mystified by, but nevertheless liking this sudden change in him.

The terrain around them changed as they rode. The barren, sparsely grassed country of the days before gave way to softer, more fertile ground, with hills in the distance that did not rise as tall and ravines that spoke of the rivers that would flow through them when the rains eventually came down.

Trees and plants of all descriptions took root in this soil and the underbrush rustled with wildlife wherever they passed. The sun shone as fiercely as ever, but twice they found watercourses which although much smaller than normal, had not yet dried up, and they were able to refill their water flasks.

Letitia was always thirsty after riding and the horses had to be watered regularly. The Slinger didn't seem to be bothered. It was as if drinking was a habit more than a need with him.

A little after noon, the Slinger led them into a grove of trees and tethered the horses near where they could graze on the rich grass. He brought out the last of the smoked rabbit-meat and shared it equally between the two of them and this time he went out to gather dry wood and twigs and he used a sulphur coated stick which he rubbed against the leather of his boot and lit a fire to boil some water.

His map told him that the green belt they were going through would soon come to and end and he decided they should make the most of it. The land is changing, he thought.

The map showed the greenery extending well past the point where they'd hit the dried wasteland.

Letitia saw that they were running out of tea she did not think that it would bother him as much as it would bother her. Somehow the Slinger seemed to be able to rise above all physical irritations and ignore them as if they were of no importance.

"Why, Letitia?" he asked after they had settled down in the shade of the trees. It was much cooler in the grove and there was a feeling of peace about the entire place. It brought pleasant memories of her youth to her and she suddenly felt very lonely and sad.

The Slinger had cleared a patch of the green grass at their feet, ringed it with stones to contain the fire, piled dry twigs high in it. The fire provided comfort. The hot food warmed her inside and made her feel more relaxed. It was so easy to think of herself as this Slinger's wife, following wherever he led.

"My parents admired the Emperor's special contingent, those not of the People, the round eyes who had come to help restore order. When they named me, they chose the name one of them mentioned. That's what they told me,"

She looked at him expectantly then but the Slinger was gazing in the middle distance.

A special insight momentarily allowed her to see herself the way he saw her, a person cast adrift in the tide of fortune. An unknown quantity whose real value had yet to be discovered and she impulsively reached out and touched his arm, ever so lightly and he looked up.

"My parents died when I was very young," she said "I was given over to the House of the Rose for training but fell out of favour with the House Master. He had me tried and publicly flogged," there was the pain of remembrance in her words now, "and exiled from the cities of the People to those held by the Ronin and round eyes."

Her words seemed to shake him and he drew his arm away from her. His thoughts went to Rei, sweet Rei, and the accursed House of the Rose and the scene he had witnessed that day with Oda and Uku and Yokito, by the lake and the consequences that simple act had precipitated that had damned them all.

Suddenly the Slinger felt terribly small and alone. The only one of his kind in a world that had changed beyond recognition to something totally different. He remembered the days spent in the Great Hall and Oku the Retainer and the love and light and warmth that had existed outside those fortified walls and he thought of the blond man and the coming of the round eyes and the passing of all that was good and right and proper and the rise of death and corruption.

He reflected that he too was round eyed, but he had passed the test of manhood. He had become one of the People. He had learnt that the Way of the Sword with its resolute acceptance of death, meant living closer to love and to life. And he thought that Musashi had been right. There had been corrupt Slingers taking up the Sword who were lost to the Way. Their minds warped by the words of the blond man and worse was yet to come.

He thought of the words of the Lady of the Reading and there was a vivid picture in his mind of the blood he had shed in the town by the desert. The women and children dying beside the men and he felt a wave of revulsion and he turned to Letitia and their eyes met.

"Why do they call you Yame?" she asked.

But the Slinger didn't answer. He gently drew her in his arms and removed their clothing and cradled her and kissed her and once more made gentle, caring love to her, for his soul was heavy and this was all the comfort he felt he could give, all he could take, the release from mortal fetters, as his mind sunk to the primal pool of instinctive sensation, and she sensed something of this, some of his pain psychically transmitted itself to her, and she broke down and this time, she cried.

Cried for herself, without knowing why, and cried for him, who was now beyond the simple capacity of tears, and cried for what was to come, which she could vaguely sense without realising it.

She clung fiercely to him and tears streamed silently from her eyes and her body was wracked with sobs and, like before, she pulled on at him, her hands gripping the thick muscles round his shoulders and his back, her legs wrapped round the small of his back as he plunged deeper into her and she felt that there was communication at some primal level taking place. An exchange of souls, of forgiveness and to a certain extent, understanding, that had nothing to do with the physical act of their coupling.

Afterwards she pressed herself in the comfort of his arms and cried herself to sleep. Cried for the pain and hurt she had suffered in her short life and the depth of some personal loss she perceived in the Slinger's mute actions, and sleep overtook her.

She woke up later, when darkness had fallen, feeling exhausted and drained, not quite comprehending what exactly had happened. The Slinger was awake, still cradling her.

"We must ride, " she said limply.

He kissed her forehead gently.

"It is too late now. We ride at dawn." he said and there was no reproach in his voice and reassured by his tenderness she drifted off to sleep again and this time she slept peacefully.

The Slinger stayed awake all night, cradling the body of the sleeping woman. He looked up through the trees and saw the stars, the familiar constellations that had guided him in his youth and he felt the passing of an age and he, too, for the first time since Rei's passing, silently wept.

Hot tears ran down his cheeks and dropped on the flattened green grass, and dripped off to soak the earth and he fought the weakness of his body that cried for the surcease of sleep and he prayed to the shadows of his ancestors. Prayed for the strength required to do what would have to be done in the days ahead.

In the morning he killed a fat squirrel which they could later have for meat and saddled the horses and they set off.

The earth was getting increasingly softer and where the grass appeared flattened the Slinger would slow down and peer closely at it looking for signs of the blond man's passage.

A few hours after they had set out, they came across horse droppings. The first they'd seen since they started chasing the blond man and the Slinger examined them. The hot morning sun had not yet dried them completely and the beetles and flies that colonised such offerings had not yet come.

The Slinger checked all around for signs of horseshoe but could fine none.

"He's only a day's ride ahead," he told Letitia and then lapsed into silence. The blond man was weakening. The Slinger sensed this. The blond man was heading for his place of power, beyond the mountains, the place where he could regenerate his energies.

It occurred to the Slinger that the blond man could be slowing down on purpose, setting another trap for him. I can defeat him, I can defeat him, I can defeat him. He told himself and felt the mantra produce the feeling of certainty which he had come to expect.

The words of the oracle and those of the lamia were fresh in his mind. There was nothing he could interpret as three days, either before or after, here, but there was a place of doom, deep beneath the earth, and they were heading for it, wind below a mountain. The blond man was heading straight for the old diamond mines. The passage that would take him across the mountains and onto the plains beyond.

There were other words the lamia had said too but the Slinger didn't want to consider them. There were many other variables affecting the future and although he had failed to find the Oracle at the Retreat he would have to depend on them if he was to save Letitia from the fate that awaited her.

He mounted his horse, "We ride all day," he told Letitia, "that way we'll make up for the lost ground."

"I'm ready," she said and he felt the pain in his breast wrought by her smile.

"Kiyah!" he spurred his horse into a gallop and he heard her following and grimly thought that he wanted no more blood of innocents on his hands.

***

Musashi moves, like a shadow, through the ranks of the students. They try to pin him down, to restrict his freedom of movements, their bamboo swords flail the air around him, but he is seemingly insubstantial.

Oku, his thick arms crossed over his massive chest, looks on and smiles. Musashi breaks up their ranks, confuses their defences, so that those trying to pin him down, to lead him onto those waiting to finish him off, get in the way of the defenders and there's a panicked melee of swirling bodies.

"Oda, the left! Stand to his left!" Rohan yells at him and Oda signals his troop to take up a position on the left of the Master. They stand ready to face him, certain that now, he'll come.

The Master is armed with a length of thin cane. Wherever it hits it leaves deep welts raised on the skin. There will be plenty of balm used later in the day to relieve the soreness. There is no sword-novice that has remained unmarked.

Rohan pushes his troop forward, their bamboo swords extended and Musashi leaps up, somersaults over the heads of Oda's troop to land on the steps leading to the battlements. Oku claps his hands with glee and smiles. He realises what the Master has done. He has changed the rules of engagement. They can only attack him two at a time now on the narrow stairs.

Effectively he has won.

Rohan groans and Oda shakes his head and kicks the dirt at his feet. In unison the sword-novices all bow.

They have lost.

Musashi, looks at the tired, sweat-streaked, flashed faces and nods his approval. He motions to Oku who flings him a large ring of keys.

The armoury!

"Time to try the short swords," he says and there's elation mixed with fear in their eyes. No more bamboo, no more bokken. Naked steel this time, this is for real.

"Don't lop off each other's tails dogspawns," cries Oku from his stand and there is some nervous laughter. A servant brings in two dozen short swords, the blades glistening in the sun.

In turn they each bend down and choose one.

"Now," Musashi tells them, "let's see if you can do this right without killing yourselves," and with a careless leap he's amongst them.

Terrified of hitting each other, they swirl to contain him, spread out to give themselves space. And the Training begins once again.

Chapter 5

The Book Of Changes

They rode hard all day and trotted through the night, alternately riding and walking to give their horses a rest and stopping only long enough for the horses to eat and drink.

The morning sun found them away from the fertile green belt and the feelings of tenderness it had engendered and in the now familiar territory of hard-baked earth and cloying dust. They were on the top of a rise looking down at the abandoned buildings of what looked like a settlement.

The buildings were made out of concrete and still stood up straight but the dust had lain thick on their flat roofs obscuring the concrete, and the glass that had covered their windows had long ago been broken.

The buildings were arranged in the shape of a horse trough with the longest of the three forming the base and the shorter two heading off it at a wide angle. A taller cylindrical structure that fanned out on top like a flower bulb on a long, thin stem, rose behind them. The structure overlooked the expanse of a flat and strangely smooth ground that seemed to stretch in long, straight lines away from the buildings.

The Slinger stared at the squat structures. There was no sign of life he could perceive.

Letitia fidgeted beside him. "Are we going down there?" The forced night ride had exhausted her. She looked pale under her brown skin and her eyes were red-rimmed and bloodshot.

Beyond the buildings, as far as the eye could see stretched the open plain and far in the distance, almost lost in the haze of heat and dust that the plain threw up into the air were the mountains that housed the diamond mines that were their destination.

The blond man was in between. Somewhere ahead.

The Slinger thought of the blond man and the closing distance and felt a constriction in his chest. The moment he feared, the moment he had desperately longed for, for so long, through so many hard nights in the past, was nearing.

The Slinger could see no sign of movement on the plain between them and the mountains. Either the blond man had reached the mountains and was crossing over to the other side, or- he had left something to delay them here, in the buildings, and could afford to wait.

He allowed his senses to quest the immediate area but there was nothing unusual to notice. The buildings radiated age. Time had passed over them erasing whatever purpose they had been expressly built for. Very far, in the distance, way beyond the buildings, there was a brief flash of metal in the sun.

It quickly disappeared.

The Slinger squinted but could see nothing.

"I am tired," Letitia announced at his side and the Slinger realised that they couldn't push their horses any further without risking losing them.

"We'll rest here, for now," he decided.

Dust had accumulated over the years and covered the wind-sheltered, hard, earth between the hill and the buildings. The horses' hoofs and their feet sank softly into it.

Little clouds of dust, like puffs of smoke, were raised by their footfalls and hang motionless about their feet, for long moments, before they fell back onto the dust-covered earth.

There was a strange feel of alieness to the entire place as if it belonged to a different era. To another world.

"They'll provide us with shade," the Slinger said, dispassionately eyeing the concrete husks they were approaching.

They came to a halt right in the middle of the courtyard formed by the layout of the buildings.

The dust-covered stretch of smooth ground they'd walked on had felt strangely hardened and flat underfoot, as if it'd been made by the powers of a god rather than the course of nature.

Everything in the immediate area felt strangely alien.

"I don't like it here," Letitia said, softly.

They crossed the flat ground and paused momentarily in front of one of the long, squat structures. It was the one on their right. The one closest to the plain beyond and the Slinger chose it in case they needed a quick getaway.

Cautiously they entered the building.

The inside looked like it had been gutted by fire.

Black soot covered the floor and the walls. Whatever furniture had been in it had been reduced to black ashes and only the metal skeleton of it remained.

Powdery glass crunched underfoot.

One of the walls had a picture. It had been painted on the concrete itself and the heat of the flames had pitted and scarred the paintwork and in patches it had flaked and the raw concrete beneath was visible.

The picture was that of a round eyed woman, dressed in wispy strips of clothing around her chest and waist. The woman was long-legged and very white and her hands must have been pushing up her hair but the paintwork had come off the wall there so that the crown of her head was missing.

The woman's arms were over her head and a playful smile, untarnished by the carnage inside the building, still touched her very red lips.

Her eyes were a vivid blue.

Underneath the woman, in faded letters of the round-eyes' speech was written in black: COCA-COLA.

"What is this place?" Letitia asked in hushed tones.

The Slinger walked around slowly trying to picture what had been there before, and failing. The toe of his boot brushed against a metal ring on the floor and he looked down.

The ring was embedded in the concrete. The Slinger rubbed away some of the soot and dust with his foot and a thin line appeared on the concrete floor. The feint outline of a trapdoor. He bent down and grasped the metal ring and braced his feet, legs spread wide apart to distribute the load equally, and he pulled.

The trapdoor came up a little with the squeaky, nerve-grating sound of rusty hinges.

Halfway up it locked. The Slinger pulled again, straining the muscles of his back, arching his body so he could push with the strength of his thighs.

For a few moments nothing happened, then with the sound of age-fatigued metal snapping the trapdoor pulled open and crashed onto the concrete floor. Dust and soot were thrown up in the air, where it struck the floor.

The Slinger peered into the dark opening. There was a flight of concrete steps leading below. From a fold in his clothing, he removed a small brown cylinder and rubbed its edge against the leather of his black boot. With a smell of sulphur the cylinder came alight. It gave off a dirty, yellow smoke that stung the eyes and made breathing difficult.

"Don't go down there," Letitia said eyeing the darkness, "please," There was real fear in her voice.

"It's all right. There is no danger there, it's been locked away too long,"

She bit her upper lip and looked at him doubtfully.

The Slinger descended the steps slowly, giving time to his eyes to adjust to the dark.

After the brightness of the sun outside there were simmering white dots dancing wherever he looked in front of him.

The room he found himself in was large and square. It opened onto another one and then another one and another after that. The network of underground chambers easily extended beyond the boundaries of the building above, possibly beyond even the boundaries of the plain itself.

The Slinger stopped and let his eyes roll over the dark, shadowy forms he could pick out in the poor, yellow light of the sulphur-filled cylinder he was holding.

There was a story here, he felt. The story of a people who had hoped for something strongly enough to build a structure that required time and skill and painstaking effort.

Death had erased it all.

This structure was all that remained now.

He sympathised with their plight. This discovery suddenly drove home to him the infinite extent of Time, the rise and passing of men and their works, the relics they left behind to mark what once must have been dark-passion fuelled hopes and dreams.

The darkness held a powerful affinity for him and he felt himself drawn to it, pulled by the strong curiosity to discover something of the world that had been and was now forgotten.

Did these buildings belong to this world, or the next? The thought crossed his mind, or the one before it? The Slinger was aware of the continuation of histories, the development of worlds that to their inhabitants' eyes had nothing in common. Time no longer followed its ordinary path. Histories were being disrupted. This was what the blond man had created. What his magic had done.

Moving cautiously, cylinder held aloft, over his head, its feeble light fighting the density of the shadows, the Slinger walked through a dark doorway and into an even greater network of chambers.

He smelled the distinct odour of sterile air, the dry, dead breath of a different world, was everywhere.

There were many small cubicles, other larger rooms, running into still others, in a seeming infinity. An underground city. He felt strangely humbled to be there. Some intervening walls had crumbled into dust to reveal what looked like beds, bathrooms in smaller cubicles alongside them.

The light of the Slinger's cylinder was lost in the expanse of each chamber. In one corner, propped up against a metal machine the purpose of which he didn't understand, the Slinger found a mummified skeleton.

The skeleton was dressed in a brown leather jacket, and boots of the same colour. His trousers were made of some kind of fabric. His jaw was hanging open and there was a cap on his head. His skin, drawn tight against the bone, desiccated, was brown and leathery looking. He seemed to be resting, leaning against the machinery by his side.

His sightless eyes looked at the doorway through which the Slinger had just entered.

The Slinger reached out tentatively and touched a gloved finger against the mummy's dried cheek. The tip of his finger went through the dried skin. It made a big hole on the side of the mummy's wizened face and then the whole thing imperceptibly shook as if waking from a long slumber, the head suddenly moved, the neck twisting to bring the dried eye-sockets in direct line with the Slinger's face and then, it dissolved into dust.

The Slinger stood there thoughtfully looking at the heap of settling dust that had once been a man.

By magic art do the works of man,
Once wrought, turn to dust again.

Oku's words, from his youth sprang into the Slinger's mind and he felt the dread of superstition clutch at his stomach and tighten his genitals with an atavistic fear. Oku had smiled at him, to take the edge off his words as he'd said it. "Trust a Lady of the Reading Rohan, but the future's only served by the strength in your sword arm and the steel of your blade," he'd admonished.

In the deathly quiet of the subterranean chamber the Slinger felt a sense of loneliness he never had experienced before assail him now.

"I miss you Oku, old friend," he whispered in the dark.

He tried to discover what the metal machine did but there was nothing to help him in this and he turned away to look into the other rooms.

Letitia's scream, thinly filtered from above, galvanized him into action.

Snapping his mind back to the present, he turned and found his way back through the series of rooms and corridors to the flight of steps he had taken to get there. He bounded up them three at a time.

Letitia was pressed against the far wall, her back pressed against the feet of the half-naked smiling woman whose name was COCA-COLA.

A round-eyed man was standing at the door, talking to her in the speech of the round eyes. The man was dressed in a leather jacket and boots, but there was no cap on his head. The man's jacket reminded the Slinger of the one the blond man wore.

His trousers were made of fabric. The Slinger thought for an instant that he looked so much like the skeleton he'd seen below, the one who'd crumbled into dust, and hesitated, superstition taking the better of him for an instant but then he saw the boots and they were different.

"Don't move," he cautioned the man in his tongue. He didn't appear to be armed.

"Hey! You speak English,"

Letitia ran behind the Slinger and looked over his shoulder at the man. "I didn't mean her no harm man," the stranger said "I just asked if she knew where I could get to a phone, or a radio or something. There seems to be nothing of the sort left here."

The Slinger stared silently at him.

"You do understand what I'm asking. Don't you?" the stranger asked. He eyed the sword at the Slinger's waist and the one strapped to his back apprehensively.

"Who are you?" the Slinger asked.

"I'm sorry. I should have introduced myself immediately- I mean I thought you-, I'm Lieutenant Joseph Brendan U.S. Clark air-base."

The Slinger continued to stare.

"I was flying over the volcano, taking readings, when it blew. Man, I thought I'd had it. Cooked my goose, you know?" the stranger laughed, but the wariness did not leave his eyes.

"Do you understand?" he asked the Slinger speaking very slowly.

"I understand you," the Slinger said to him and turned to Letitia and said "Let's go outside,"

They filed past the door. The stranger reluctantly following them.

"I need to get to a radio, or a phone," he said "they'll be looking for me now. I have to report in to base."

"What happened?" the Slinger asked.

"What happened? Man! What happened? The volcano blew man, that's what happened. It just blew its top. I was passing right over it. Man it was hell, never seen nothing like it, that's what happened. I had barely had enough time to jettison. That's why I must call in. They'll never find the plane in that mess and if they do they may think I've bought it."

The Slinger looked at the stranger for a long time, trying to find a reference that would help him decipher his words. He could understand what the man was saying but no sense seemed to come out of it. There had been no volcanoes for a thousand years and the man had intimated that he had just been flying over one.

The Slinger found that hard to believe.

"You say you're lost?" he asked.

"Man, I told you, my bird came down. I just need to find a telephone."

The Slinger sat down in the shadow thrown by the walls of the building. He tried to piece together the man's appearance with the actions of the blond man. The blond man was nearer. This man had now appeared. The man's clothes were not unlike the blond man's but that meant very little.

The Slinger remembered in the time beyond, before the desert crossing, he had memories of his father in similar clothes. He hoped that meant that the changes that the world was undergoing could be acting as much against the blond man as for him.

"First we'll eat," the Slinger said and motioned for the stranger to sit down.

The stranger sat down, "OK by me Joe, as long as I get to a phone some time," he said.

Working methodically, the Slinger entered a couple of buildings in turn, came back from one of them carrying some pieces of wood, along with some other thinner pieces, harder than wood, made of a material that was not metal.

He piled them all together and used one of his sulphur coated sticks to light a fire. The dry wood caught immediately and thick, choking smoke started pouring from the pile.

The Slinger and Letitia backed away from it.

"Hey man! That's plastic! You can't cook food over this!" the stranger yelled, he kicked at the fire, removed the smoking pieces that were not wood and stomped on them to put out the flames. He looked at the Slinger and the woman looking at him impassively and opened his arms in a gesture of helplessness.

"You really don't understand, do you?" he asked but he got no reply.

The Slinger brought out the skinned squirrel he had killed earlier that morning. It would barely do for three. He skewered it through a thin metal wire and stretched it over the fire, to cook.

The stranger realised how hungry he was. His watch and compass had been damaged when his parachute had landed and he had walked for miles trying to find a place to call from. He realised he had no way of finding the place he fell into any more than he knew where he was.

Despite the swords and the sullen looks the man in black with the big silver badge pinned to his chest, looked friendly enough, he decided. And the woman was exceptionally pretty. Some sort of Oriental half-caste, a bit of Japanese thrown in there probably.

He ate the pieces of meat they offered him and drunk the refreshing water from the flask, he tried to marshal his thoughts. The day was hot but he didn't want to remove his leather jacket. He had a colt .45 in a shoulder holster and, he felt, that the sight of the gun could complicate matters unnecessarily.

"How were you lost?" the Slinger asked.

"My compass was broken and my watch." He saw that the Slinger didn't understand and tried to explain. "I have no way of telling the time, or the direction I travel in. I thought this was a base, but it's been abandoned, the air-strip's all covered over." he indicated with a sweep of his arm the smooth long lines stretching through the plain, behind the buildings.

The strange man kept talking, explaining, but the Slinger was not listening. His mind was occupied by thoughts, images, half-heard rumours whispered by the People, about the men that had come from the sky. The round eyes who obeyed Rohan's father, who rode with the Emperor and carried a gun.

"In a tight spot, there's nothing like a good revolver Rohan, remember that," his father had said.

Rohan had looked at the small, black weapon that nestled in his father's hand and thought of its impersonal nature compared to a sword.

"The sword is all right son, but we must find a way to get you one of these." his father had hefted the gun, before returning it to its niche at his waist.

Rohan had looked at him enquiringly, there was a whole mystery hidden behind his father's words, an explanation to their being with the People, the sudden appearance of other round eyes, much like them and yet so different.

Rohan had waited but his father had never explained. He had truly hoped that one day he'd be told that the rumours that they'd fallen out of the sky were false, lies spread by superstitious peasants.

The Slinger looked at the strange man, who had brought back all these memories.

"You don't really care I'm lost," the man said and there suddenly was a tone in his voice that the Slinger couldn't analyse, but was the simple need for help of one person, reaching out to the feelings of a fellow being.

There was something akin to the message of the underground passages and their quenched world in the strange man's yearning and the Slinger responded.

"Perhaps The Book will help you," he said. The Slinger reached into a pocket and pulled out a parched fold of leather, faded and badly worn at the edges. He laid it out on the ground, between himself and the stranger and took out three coins, each with a hole in the middle. He balanced them in the palm of his hand, feeling their weight, before tossing them. "Ask your questions," he said.

The stranger looked at him. His face showed anxiety. "What-"

"Quietly. In your head."

The Slinger tossed the coins. Six times, once for each line of the hexagram.

Throughout this procedure the stranger stared quietly. He looked like he had gone into some kind of shock. "Is this the I Ching?" he asked finally. He had heard of the Book of Changes, knew some guys back on base that used it a lot, meditated. He looked very uncertain.

"It is The Book. Ask and you shall receive, so it is stated." the Slinger said to him.

Letitia nodded encouragingly. She didn't like this stranger. His presence unsettled her too much, reminded her that the Slinger and she were not travelling on business of land or law, but were hunting a sorcerer. She didn't want to be reminded of that.

Perhaps The Book's answer would drive the stranger away she decided. Without a horse the stranger couldn't ride with them and the Slinger had said the blond man was near. Surely he wanted to chase him as fast as possible.

"I am not as skilled as a Lady of the Reading," the Slinger said, "but you are in urgent need, for you it may suffice," he looked down to see what the coins had drawn up.

"Hexagram number four, do you know the meaning?" the stranger shook his head negatively.

"Innocence," the Slinger said and then he quoted from memory: "Innocence gets through successfully. Though you do not seek the innocent yourself, the innocent seek you. Muddling is not informative. It is advantageous to be correct."

He sat back feeling puzzled. The Reading connected to the previous one, the one given him by the Lady of the Reading in the nameless town by the desert where he had been forced to spill the blood of innocents to get out of the blond man's trap. He thought of the associated image of a spring emerging from under a mountain that he'd learnt: *innocence! Cultured people nurture character by fruitful action.* What did it mean?

Was he to be responsible for this strange man who claimed to have come from the sky?

Was this the blond man's doing? An attempt to slow him down when he was getting so near?

"What does it mean?" the stranger asked, clearly he didn't understand either.

"What was your question?" the Slinger asked him.

"I asked how do I get out of here," he said.

"In innocence there is danger below a mountain. Stopping at danger there is innocence. Innocence gets through by successful action at the right time." explained the Slinger, he pointed to the distant mountains.

"There! In those mountains lieutenant Joseph Brendan is the way out you seek."

"Is he going to travel with us?" Letitia had read the hexagram too.

"Yes,"

"But how? He has no horse,"

"The horses are tired," the Slinger said "we'll take it in turns. He can first ride mine."

Chapter 6

The Blond Man

He has come to see his father.

The journey has taken him an entire day and he can feel his muscles aching from the long ride.

The Emperor's Keep is every bit as imposing as he remembered, with guards lining the battlements, their spears shining in the sun.

There are peasants around the thick base of the outer walls, hawking their wares and colourfully dressed people move in and out and Rohan drinks in the sights and the smells and the sounds, so different from the sterile austerity of the Great Hall, and he feels the thrum of the place from which the Empire is ruled and the word of the Law goes out to the masses.

"Do you want a drink sirhan? A drink for a server of the sword?" a wizened old woman thrusts a bottle of something pungent at him and he backs away.

Server of the sword. Of course, there's a short sword at his waist now: A companion sword. No different to the ones worn by the merchants, or some of the more daring peasants. But to him it's a potent symbol with a worth deeper than its face value.

He's no longer just a mere sword-novice.

He has made progress. The Way of the Sword is still long and painful but he has taken his first step on the path that leads to it.

He declines the old woman's offer with a curt shake of his head and turns to find his way through the crowd.

"Meat? Fresh meat only here!" someone else shouts behind him.

There are smells of spices he's never tasted before and out of the corner of his eye he sees a coarse-looking man of enormous girth stand on a wooden platform and wave a thick stick with a bell attached to it, to attract the crowd's attention. He's holding a pretty girl by the hand, and as people gather he turns and whips the cape that covers her away and displays her naked body to the crowd.

There's a murmur from many throats in the air.

"Three silver pieces! Three silver pieces!" Rohan hears him yell, "The girl's hardly been touched, three silver pieces a time!"

Grubby male hands reach towards the girl's bare legs and she shrinks back from the crowd, until the fat man jerks her hand and she's pushed forward again.

The press of the crowd presently grows a little uncomfortable for Rohan. He's not accustomed to such closeness, with so many people about and at the first opportunity he slips out of the throng and heads for the Great Gate.

There are only two guards on duty at the outer portals and they recognise his face and detain him.

"Your father is consulting with the Emperor young master. Can't you come back another time?"

Here at last he's on familiar footing. "My leave expires today," he says "I have to return to the Great Hall or face the wrath of the Master,"

The two guards confer with each other, the red crest of the Imperial dragon emblazoned upon their chests, shines as they move. They know all about restrictions and they know the young round-eyes isn't lying. Great Hall strictures are not to be contravened, and in the past they've had the chance to see Musashi's wrath in action, at the barracks.

They sympathise.

"If you're quick," one of the says at last, then: "But if anyone asks you never went through this gate,"

Rohan gives them a quick bow and a smile and runs past the tradesmen unloading their carts on the Keep courtyard, heading towards the Keep proper and the great steps that'll take him inside.

He goes through the long, dark passages, admiring the weapons he sees on the walls comparing them with the one he is carrying.

There are swords of different lengths. Swords with names, and stories of valour. The men who wielded them are legends every sword-novice knows about. They're Slingers who have mastered their shadows. Rohan knows the names of these Slingers by heart, they are names the clans revere.

He passes a door that is slightly ajar and he hears voices coming from within.

"You must let him know!"

"I cannot, what you ask...it would surely kill him,"

"You will obey me in this!"

One of the voices is suddenly raised in anger and Rohan recognises it as one familiar to him.

Though it's improper he pauses and peers through the crack of the door and his shock at what he sees within is such that without thinking he opens it and enters.

Yukio is sitting in a chair facing the blond man. The Emperor's seer is dressed in the same clothes Rohan had last seen him in. Yukio is dressed in white, pure white. Her face is bowed in shame and her eyes are red with crying.

"Rohan! What are you doing here?" Yukio is startled to see him.

Rohan says nothing.

"Ah, the round eyed pup!" the blond man smiles, "Come sniffing round for something? Or is your sex-crazed friend rotting in a cell again, his brain located between his thin legs as always?"

Rohan goes deep red at the insult but doesn't rise to the bait. "Yukio, you all right?" he asks and Yukio nods quickly. Her eyes won't look at him still.

"Does my father know you're here?"

"No! And you mustn't tell him," she says and there's anxiety colouring her voice.

Rohan feels the dark bite of suspicion. Something which he can't understand is going on.

"Shall I call a guard?" Rohan asks.

The blond man smiles at this. "She has no need of guards young pup," he sneers.

"Give us a proper Reading seer or shut your lying mouth," says Rohan and there is an adult firmness in his voice and Yukio wails.

Rohan looks at her. He doesn't understand what he's done wrong.

The blond man is now trembling with fury. "A Reading? You want a Reading you pup? Very well then, a Reading it shall be,"' and he stretches his hands towards the sky and his blue eyes darken and widen and he brings his hands in a wide arc to meet in front of him, fingertips touching and his voice when he speaks drips with venomous power.

Rohan can feel it, but he refuses to be terrified. He brings his right hand to his short sword and grips the handle until his knuckles whiten, but he holds his fear at bay.

He has been taught that only a Lady of the Reading can lay a curse on a Slinger. The Master has warned that fear is the weapon you give your opponent to bludgeon you to death with, so he withholds his fear. Denies the blond man whatever small victory it would give him.

"The Lamb shall rear to rend the wolves," the blond man says and Yukio shakes her head and unshed tears fill her pretty dark eyes. "Those last taught shall be the first to go. No one will make the rites any more. There'll be no more Slinger Lore. Nor will there be anyone to uphold the Law."

Satisfied the blond man, lowers his hands and stares triumphantly at Rohan whose face has gone white.

But it is rage, not fear that makes Rohan slit his eyes, and as the blond man stares the boy smiles back icily. A terrifying, narrow smile that unsettles the blond man so much that he makes the sign of the horns at him and involuntarily takes a step back, as if he's seen his own death in that smile.

"Go dogspawn!" he says and Rohan runs out of the room and Yukio, beautiful Yukio, breaks down and cries and her pain makes the blond man smile again, though now not even he is sure what has been accomplished by this unpredictable instant in time.

Rohan runs out of the Emperor's Keep, down the long, wide steps of stone, past the guards with their dragon emblem and shiny spears, past the inner courtyard where specially ordered goods are being unloaded and past the killing ground, the carefully prepared area where the Emperor's archers from the parapets would dispose of anyone foolhardy enough to breach the main gate and enter.

There has been a brief moment of clarity within his young mind when he has been outside himself, and he's seen the role of the blond man.

He has seen Yukio cry. The feeling of unrest and unsettlement that has brought him to the Keep in search of his father, suddenly finds a positive course of action to channel itself into.

He turns his decision over in his mind and feels the aura of absolute certainty radiating from it. The blond man's words have formed a picture inside his head. A picture of terrifying clarity. And it has given him the conviction he needed to know what to do.

In the brief moment of revelation that was granted him, Rohan has seen the Slinger clans destroyed and the Great Hall given up to flames. He has seen the bitter passing of the Slinger clans: no more sword warriors roaming the land, the Law forgotten, all peace lost, and the Great Keep in ruins. He has, in short, seen the fall of all he holds dear. And he has also felt that all this can be changed.

At a run he reaches the stables, vaults lightly over the barrier guarding the gate and saddles the nearest charger. The stable master comes running, three stable lads yelling behind him, but Rohan has no time to explain. He throws them a silver coin, the only money he has, and pushing his horse to jump over the barrier, he rides off.

Soon it'll be night.

He rides wildly, pushing the charger at the top of its speed, urging it to go as fast as it can and the beautifully trained animal obeys.

He rides all through the night and dawn finds him outside the Great Hall's battlements, with his charger trembling beneath him in exhaustion and sweat running down the inside of his thighs, where they're pressed tight against the animal's huffing flanks.

He dismounts quickly certainty holding his fatigue at bay, and leading the charger by the reins knocks on the heavy armoured door of the Great Hall.

"Open up!" he yells at the top of his voice. The sun is barely up and he has no time to waste.

"Identify yourself," cries a thin voice.

It is the early morning watch, the shift given to acolytes and young sword-novices and Rohan bangs impatiently on the door again.

"Open up or be damned young fools! I am Rohan!" he cries.

There's the scrape of wood as a watch-hole is pushed back at eye-level, the thin face of a young acolyte peering though it.

"Rohan!" he cries, "What are you doing back so early? Your leave was good for three days!"

The great thick, wooden bolts are pulled back quickly and one half of the great portal is swung open to admit him and his charger.

Three uncertain young faces hover about him.

"Prepare the Arena!" Rohan says by way of explanation and their eyes widen but they recognize the authority in his voice and without another word they each bow and go, leaving the gate unguarded.

Feeling the recklessness of the moment Rohan throws his head back and laughs. The blond man has said that there'll be no more Slinger Lore and those last taught shall be the first to go and now Rohan is going to prove him wrong.

He's spent long hours lying awake at night studying the Changes predicted by The Book, a lot of the messages have been beyond him, but he knows the power single, individual acts have to negate Time. He's suddenly determined to teach the seer a lesson.

He runs through the compound and the novice quarters to where Oda and the others are still sleeping and he pours cold water over them.

"Rohan! You horse-turd! We'll get you for this!" cries Oda.

"Come to the Arena!" Rohan yells at their sleep-fogged faces and they understand and their eyes suddenly go wide and they start dressing hurriedly, choosing the red of ceremony over the yellow of practice for they see the importance of this.

Rohan is only fifteen.

The entire compound is soon in an uproar.

Some attendants have rushed to waken the Master Swordsman, Musashi, and they have found the sword saint, awake at his calligraphy, penning a poem in fierce, broad strokes.

"Senki!" he explains to them: war-spirit, and the attendants bow and retreat for they fear the Master and somehow sense that he knows exactly what's happening without needing to be told.

The Arena, fills slowly. The floor is quickly strewn with loose straw and oil is carefully spilled in places. There'll be purpose-laid treacherous patches on the arena floor which will prove the undoing of the careless this day.

Rohan has gone yelling to the Retainer's quarters where Oku reposes, two nubile young girls flanking him on either side. "Oku wake up, you son of a pig!" he yells at him the ceremonial insult, kicking the door open and Oku, whose left arm is ready to throw his knife should there prove to be an assailant at the door, lies back and covers his face with a thick, hairy arm and groans.

"The young fool. He should have waited," he tells the girls and there is real sadness in his voice.

Musashi is the last to come to the Arena. He sits at the centre of the seats, the place of honour specially prepared for him and he wears the habitual fierceness that casts a grim gloom on his face.

Rohan appears at one end. He is barefoot and stripped to the waist. The young musculature developed from the hours spent in the practice hall glistens with the oil the servants who prepared him have rubbed on. He has only a length of thin, flexible cane, in one hand.

"Rohan, you fool! You haven't got your bokken," Oda yells at him but Rohan ignores him.

He looks at the twin service doors, the one facing east, that will open for the winner to emerge wearing the long sword. The other facing west which if he loses he'll follow, to join the ranks of the Ronin, the wave men, the flotsam that clutter the empire and live on the fringe of the Law.

It's no choice. And the blond man probably knew it well, when he issued his terrible curse. No more Slinger Lore! No more Law!

We shall see, Rohan thinks, we shall see!

He then stops.

At the far end, the doors open and Oku appears. He's dressed in full war armour and there's a helmet on his head. He wears the full set of two swords, spear, bow and arrow and as he comes in he looks immense. An incarnation of Hatjiman himself, the god of war. The students and acolytes fall quiet, in awe.

The fierce Musashi grins approvingly.

"Choose your weapons," says Oku ceremoniously and Musashi leans forward expectantly. This is the moment that will decide the fight. The best students choose the bokken, those who are frightened choose the spear, or the long sword.

There has never been a younger challenger. Of the People or otherwise. The scribes also lean forward, eager to record his words, their feathered quills quivering in sudden expectation.

Rohan whips the thin bamboo cane through the air. "I have chosen," There is total silence.

Out of the corner of his eye Rohan catches the glances of disbelief exchanged by the acolytes, sees Oda strike his forehead in dismay.

"Let the contest begin then," says Oku and takes the first step forward.

The Retainer flings his spear forcing Rohan to dodge and move to one side. It has been a slow throw intended to make Rohan change position rather than hurt him.

The Arena is rectangular, and Oku aims to corner Rohan at the upper end and dispose of him there.

As the Retainer advances, Rohan stops. He drops his hands near his waist, bends his knees, body straight and waits. Oda and Uku see this and nudge each other, the Master, glowering leans forward. The lad is too lightly armed, this is a contest of near death, to tap the Retainer with the bamboo stick will not be enough.

Rohan holds his ground, arms slightly extended to either side, away from his body. He has adopted the classic pose, Happo Biraki: open on all eight sides. There is no known opening for an attack to such position. Oku will have to charge him.

Rohan feels every inch of his body, every hair follicle on his head, the grating of straw beneath his bare feet. His body has become his weapon and he has become one with the world.

He is ready to move.

With a war-cry Oku attacks, he brings his long sword down on Rohan, but Rohan is no longer there. He has twisted and turned so that his back is to the Retainer and he now pushes the thin length of cane hard, between the plates of the armour, where the man's genitals are.

Oku grunts loudly but the blow doesn't stop him. He slaps Rohan aside, sends him reeling away from him and now the long sword is flourished again and Rohan has to roll on the straw, desperately trying to manoeuvre the Retainer towards the oily patch where his footing will be compromised.

Oku sees it at the very last minute and he steps over it, overreaching by a fraction and for an instant he's vulnerable. Reflexively he brings his sword down to the side where Rohan's body is but Rohan has rolled away and the blade just cuts his extended bamboo cane in half.

It gives Rohan the time he needs. He leaps to his feet and twirls inside Oku's attack, his body closely cleaves to the path the long sword has taken as Oku lifts it for his next attack.

It is a flawless performance. The students' jaws drop in admiration and Musashi, the Master Swordsman, raises his bushy eyebrows in wonder at the audacity of it. He, better than anybody present there, understands what Rohan has achieved.

It is the no-mind that comes with the resolute acceptance of death. Rohan has defeated his fear, embraced death like a brother, and whatever the Retainer may do now, to stop Rohan, he'll first have to kill him.

Musashi feels his heart swell with pride.

Rohan stops inside the big man's defences and with consummate accuracy and skill, pushes the remaining half of the bamboo stick through the face guard's opening into Oku's eye and, in the same movement, swirls away.

The Retainer grunts with the pain and drops to one knee, his long sword drops from his hand as he clutches at the stick in his eye. Rohan kicks at him: neck, shoulder and throat where only the pads protect him and the Retainer staggers.

"Yield!" Rohan yells but the Retainer has still got plenty of fight left in him. He grasps the bamboo stick with one hand and pulls it out of his eye, its splintered end bloodied and with the other he picks up his long sword again.

He sweeps the blunt end of it in an arc that unexpectedly catches Rohan at the side of the ribs with a crack and the breath goes out of him. The skin is split open and thin, watery blood streams down his side. Rohan's face goes white.

The students watch with baited breath.

The Retainer rises to his feet. The pain from his dead eye must be intense, for his body wavers slightly but he's not going to make it easy for the boy. He swings his head this way and that, tracking Rohan with his good eye, a feral grimace on his face.

Rohan ducks beneath the next swing, moves to the Retainer's blinded side and kicks savagely at the knee, the Retainer's leg buckles.

This time Rohan doesn't hesitate.

He gets behind the Retainer, wraps his forearm against his windpipe and bracing himself to take the strain pulls with all his young body's strength.

"Yield!" he grants through clenched teeth.

Oku struggles to regain his balance fighting against the unbalancing weight of his armour and the force exerted by Rohan. He knows the hold for what it is. Unless he gets out of it he'll black out.

"Yield!" yells Rohan again pulling back as hard as he can. His ribs, where the flat of the sword has struck him are on fire and he knows that if the Retainer manages to break his hold his chances of success will vanish. He shifts his stance and brings his entire body's weight to bear, pulling against the Retainer's windpipe.

With pin-pricks dancing in front of his eyes, Oku hoarsely says: "I yield, Rohan. I yield Slinger." and, as Rohan at last releases his grip, the Retainer slumps forward in relief, blood streaming profusely from his blinded eye.

The students rush forward. They surround Rohan, lift him to their shoulders.

"Well done Slinger!" they hail him.

They're still dazed by the contest they've just stood witness to.

"Rohan, you hardly left anything for us to see to. He's only got one eye now." says Oda slapping him in the back.

Rohan grunts back, trying to overcome his own pain.

He's a Slinger and he's only fifteen!

Attendants come bearing a stretcher, preparing to take Oku away.

"Wait," Oku says. His voice is barely audible. "Before you go, word must travel to the other clans. It is right that a round eye has passed the test of manhood. But unnecessary challenges become the cause of needless bloodshed. You should not have to worry about that. Post the announcements, in the villages and the City, there's a new Slinger in the Emperor's service. Then sent word to the Emperor, I shall be unable to train his personal guard for a while, explain why."

Rohan understands, nods. Oku is right. "I shall do it myself." he says, and he thinks to himself: the blond man will know now, the curse is broken.

"And get those ribs seen to," Oku mumbles before he's taken away, the attendants straining under the weight of the stretcher.

There is now a silence.

The scribes wait expectantly, their quills poised.

Musashi stands up. Descends the steps. Everybody parts respectfully, making way. He stops in front of Rohan and from his belt he gives him a key. It is large and on it is embossed the crane and the eagle, Musashi's personal crest.

"Go to the armoury," he says "choose your long sword. The eastern gate shall be open for three days and nights. At the end of the three I want you back here, for the ceremony."

Hiding the pain he feels from his side, Rohan bows. His heart is thrilled. He's a Slinger, he's earned the right to wear the long sword, roam the countryside, go into the City's brothels. He's proved the blond man wrong. The Slinger Lore is not yet lost. He is the first, the first of those who are being taught to uphold the Law.

Little does he know he's also going to be the last.

***

Lieutenant Joseph Brendan rode first and the Slinger walked by his side. Letitia sullenly brought up the rear. As he rode, Brendan kept casting sidelong glances at the strange man in black with his long black hair and his two swords and kept trying to understand what exactly had happened to himself.

It was like he was going crazy. Like he was caught in a waking nightmare he could not get out of. Only this, as far as he could tell, was for real.

The strange words of the I Ching, kept coming up in his mind like a prophecy. The
man in black had been very solemn in his belief of what that hexagram, conjured up with the three coins had predicted.

Brendan didn't know what to make of it all, but if it was going to be his ticket out he was willing to risk anything. Besides he didn't think himself to be in great physical danger. He still had his colt .45 and three full clips of ammunition and he had yet to see a sword beat a gun.

The solemnity and sense of purpose he felt in the man in black, made Brendan like him, almost despite himself and the woman was undeniably beautiful. He thought of the comic-books he had read as a youth, the air-force pilot who had gone through an opening of the earth at the poles and had entered another world where he'd become a Warlord, the only person to wield a hand-gun in a primitive, savage world.

His mind toyed with fantasies.

He was pretty sure that he was no longer in the Philippines and he toyed with the idea that he wasn't even on Earth, at least not the Earth he'd so recently flown a plane in.

"What's in the mountains?" Brendan finally broke the silence, speaking to the Slinger.

"Mines. Diamond mines."

"King Solomon's?" he joked but the name meant nothing to the Slinger and he didn't respond.

"How will this get me home?"

"I don't know. The words of The Book are not always clear. They require the knowledge of a Lady of the Reading in order to be completely understood. The Book however is never wrong."

"Do the mines go under the mountains?"

"Yes."

"What's on the other side?"

"A plain. A river. The lost home of the Ainu."

The Lieutenant didn't understand and the Slinger felt this. This strange man who claimed to have come from the sky knew so little about everything, that perhaps he had told the truth.

"The Ainu are an old race," the Slinger explained "they lived in a land where the water never stopped flowing and the crops grew tall. They were driven from their homeland by a fierce enemy. Ever since, they make their homes near mountain. Surviving on the food they levy from those who work the mines and the tithes they earn for providing protection from marauders."

"Are they dangerous?"

The Slinger considered the nature of the question. Danger could take many forms. For that matter, the very absence of the Ainu might herald a far greater danger than he and this strange man could ever hope to deal with.

"The mines have not been worked for a long time. The Ainu have probably moved on."

"Oh,"

"What's he saying?' Letitia asked from behind. She didn't like this stranger, she'd seen the familiar look in his eyes when he looked at her, the look that her training at the House of the Rose had taught her to recognize and use.

It was the same look that Ronin and round eyes had levelled at her time and again when she'd found herself without protection in the town with no name and she remembered only too clearly the indignities she'd been made to suffer there in the name of survival.

She also resented the fact that she no longer was the only one riding with the Slinger.

"He's thinking of how to get back where he came from," the Slinger said to her.

"Ask him about the blond man. He may know something." she suggested.

The Slinger thought about it. If the blond man had sent this Brendan here, then maybe Brendan knew him, or of him.

"There is a man riding ahead," the Slinger said and Brendan perked up at this.

"Another man? Where?"

"He's half a day ahead, maybe less. The distance is closing."

"Are you after this man?"

"Yes."

Brendan digested this piece of information, carefully asked: "What's he like? This man you're chasing?"

"Blond. With hair long, like mine and a beard and eyes of hard blue, like cold fire. He wears a leather jacket, brown like yours with teeth at the edges and there are red wings on the breast. And he's always dressed in a white silk shirt and brown leather trousers and boots of the same colour."

The description seemed to strike a chord of recognition in the stranger's eyes, "What's his name? This man's of yours?"

"He hasn't got a name. Some people know him as the Render, others call him the Seer. Still others know him simply as the Traitor,"

Brendan scratched his head. "If I didn't know better, the description of the clothes and looks, sounds like a man I know. My immediate superior, Lt. Col. Eversteen Russel, the man who ordered the flight over- No. It can't be."

The Slinger said simply: "The blond man has many powers, but he is weakening. It could be that your being here is something he has done."

After that the Slinger fell silent and they stopped only once to change so that the Slinger now rode and Brendan walked.

Brendan felt that each step he took removed him that much further from the world he'd known and placed him deeper in the fabric of life of this strange realm. The weight of the colt on the inside of his jacket gave him the only reassurance that he wasn't dreaming.

Perhaps I'm lying hurt somewhere, he thought, my body badly burnt and unconscious and my mind is giving me this story to keep me occupied. Or perhaps I'm dead, this could be Heaven, or more likely, Hell.

Keep this up and you will go crazy, he eventually admonished himself. There was no denying the reality of the man in black, but the description of this blond man he was chasing? Did people in dreams get tired and have to ride on horses to relax?

He thought about it and couldn't really see why they shouldn't have to if the dream was to maintain consistency. He suddenly wished he hadn't left his damaged watch and compass behind, but when he'd seen the airfield from afar he'd thought he was all right. Rescue was at hand.

I never thought the I Ching was anything more than a parlour game, he thought to himself, and pressed his lips in a thin determined line. Come what may he was determined to get out of this mess alive.

Chapter 7

The Mountains

Rohan is dressed in Slinger black. The other students, his friends, are all gathered in the training room of the Great Hall. The very same place where so long ago Musashi, first noticed a round-eyes fighting like a wild-cat against almost impossible odds, and still managing to come through.

He carries the two swords now, one at the waist, one strapped to his back. As he walks he feels the weight of the armaments secreted in his clothing. The herbs and the powders, the potions for making others sleep and the medicines for healing all but the deepest of wounds. The shuriken needles and the blades, too thin to be felt once the killing starts, and the chains for strangling the unwary.

Alone, armed like this, Rohan stands in the middle of the Training Hall and the four great drums, one at each corner begin their slow, rhythmical beat.

The lesser drums now take up the primitive rhythm. A whole array of them lining all the back wall. The acolytes' hands blur as they strike, and their faces shine with sweat.

Rohan wishes his father were here, but his father is again on the road, with the Emperor. His mother, like all women, barred from attending, the Great Hall.

Now the students clap their hands and stamp their feet in time to the savage drum-beat.

In one corner stands the bulk of Oku, the Retainer, a black leather patch covering his left eye, clapping along with the others.

Rohan's eyes manage to catch his gaze and Oku grins and his good eye glints fierce encouragement.

Musashi, enters the hall, the drums beat a little louder, the Master is solemn. He walks slowly, ceremoniously towards Rohan standing alone in the middle of the hall. The Master has done this many times, though never for one so young. He times his steps to arrive in front of Rohan just as the drums reach a crescendo and stop.

There is absolute silence.

Rohan kneels.

The Master puts his hand on Rohan's left shoulder. His voice is gravely when he says: "The Way of the Sword is the Way of Heaven."

A thousand mouths repeat his words, Rohan's breath catches in his throat. He has dreamed of this occasion a million times.

"The Sword is the Way of the manifold path. Nirvana is attained through the practice of the Sword. The body and spirit are only extensions of the Sword. The mind resides within the paths of the Sword. In the Sword reigns Peace. In the Sword reigns Happiness. In the Sword reigns Justice. Blest are those who walk in the path of the Sword. May the Sword guide them to an honourable life. May the Sword guide them to a timely death."

With the ceremonial prayer over, a student walks up to the Master. He drops to one knee in front of him, eyes lowered to the floor. In his hand he holds a silk covered tray.

The silk is purest black. In the centre of the tray shines a silver star. The imperial dragon is embossed upon its face.

The Master takes the star and the student bows low and leaves. The Master then turns to Rohan.

"With this star you're no longer round eyes," he says and everybody waits with baited breath. This is not part of the ceremony.

Oku nods his head in complete agreement. They have spent long hours discussing this, he and the Master. Rohan is a round eyes, the first, the only one, to ever become a Slinger. It is important that enmities are laid to rest. It is important that the Slinger clans know this.

With a loud clear voice Rohan repeats: "With this star I am no longer round eyes."

The Master now begins to recite the Slinger oath of duty.

"With this star you join the People.

"To administer the Law in the name of the Emperor.

"And see that all justice is done."

Rohan repeats the words.

The Master now pins the silver star to Rohan's chest and the drums start their primitive crescendo and the students clap and stamp their feet in time and big Oku grins madly and the Master gives Rohan the ultimate accolade:

"Everybody knows you as Rohan," he says and everyone strains to hear over the roll of the drums. They know what's coming next. He's to be given a name. One chosen by the Master and the clan.

It'll be the name his deeds will be remembered by and the one which all Slinger clans shall know and accept in the stories and tales of their lore.

"To the Slingers you are now Yame, the Shadow."

Rohan stands up and Musashi, the sword saint, the Master of the Great Hall, who has seen dozens of Slingers of many clans pass through its doors, takes Rohan by the shoulders and hugs him fiercely.

A ceremonial bowl of water is brought, the water has been drawn from a well blessed by a Lady of the Reading. The Master dips his right hand in the bowl, scoops up some water and sprinkles Rohan's face with it.

The hall explodes in cries of jubilation. The drums are beating faster than ever. Rohan sets his face into a mask to hide his emotions. He can do no less. He has just been christened. He is now formally a Slinger.

***

They reached the base of the mountains just before dusk. "We'll go on," the Slinger said, "There's little time to lose." He held himself in rigid control. There was a palpable alertness about him now which both his companions could sense.

"In the darkness we won't be able to get very far," Brendan said "and the mountain face looks steep from here,"

The Slinger stared hard at him. "We are close to the blond man, very close. There will be danger. The more we dally the greater the risk."

"I have this," Brendan said and from the shoulder holster of his jacket he pulled out the colt .45. The Slinger didn't look impressed. His father had lived by the gun all his life, and he'd died by the sword. The Slinger pushed the unwanted thought away.

Brendan was about to explain the power of a hand-gun when the Slinger spoke.

"Guns are slow. They have to be loaded, one shot at a time and their direction of aim lies in a single line. There is no art to killing with a gun. Anyone can do it. The sword can cut from anywhere and its power comes from within the wielder,"

"This is a semi-automatic," Brendan said waving the gun around. "Thirteen shots and I have three more clips for this babe."

The Slinger shrugged. McQuaid had had a gun, back in the town by the desert. It had done him no good. The Emperor had outlawed all guns, they impoverished the soul.

Round eyes today used guns, the Slinger knew well, but back then only his father had carried one and had only ever used it in the Emperor's service. His father had never understood the way of the Sword, if he had, the Slinger thought, perhaps he wouldn't have perished so easily. This Brendan will bear watching the moment any action starts the Slinger decided.

"Unsaddle your horse," he ordered Letitia "we'll leave the horses here. We may need to use them again."

"We are going to climb? Aren't we?" she asked.

"The blond man has,"

Letitia unsaddled her horse. Tethered the animal to a nearby bush.

Her face was lost in thought for a moment, as if she listened to a voice only she could now hear. Then, as if having debated for a long time and finally reached a decision she came back to stand by the Slinger.

"The blond man gave me my fate," she said looking up at his face and her voice was pitched higher than usual with fright. "Karma cannot always be escaped, it is perhaps best I don't come with you,"

The Slinger contemplated it without expression. He was being asked to choose again, made responsible for future outcomes he couldn't control. He didn't want that, to leave her behind, unprotected, would be consigning her to death. Unbidden, the vision the lamia had revealed to him played itself in his mind and there was a leaden weight on his chest when he said: "There are no waves in the mountains."

Brendan had sat on a rock and was watching them. He had his gun out and was cleaning it, checking and re-checking the clip.

"Nevertheless, I want you to know," Letitia moved closer to the Slinger, she could feel the heat rising off his body, his presence was like a palpable pressure on her heart. "I love you. I always loved you, from the moment I saw you, when you came off the desert. I knew it then. Impossibly, I thought to myself, that I knew it."

The Slinger gently put his hands on her shoulders. He thought of other partings, of sallies into danger, of Rie seeing him off from the Keep. He felt hollow inside, unable to offer anything more than his anger and anguish. What could he say to this woman who had followed him?

He drew his short sword and gave it to her. "You'll need this." he said.

The sun had now set and a bright moon was out. The mountain face glowed eerily and its summit rose above them. There had to be an entrance to the mines somewhere, the Slinger thought and he caught a half-glimpse of something shining halfway up the face.

He remembered the glimmer of metal he'd seen when he was near the buildings and squinted but the play of shadows and rocks revealed nothing more. I can defeat him, I can defeat him, I can defeat him, he said to himself.

He thought perhaps he should prepare himself, call on *Kobudera*, Slinger magic, chance another journey through the spirals and share the sleep of his ancestors, but he exercised no control on the planes his spirit travelled in and there was little time left for the meditation it required. Besides, the spirals, though saving him from the desert, had also weakened him the last time he'd used them. They'd made him lose control of his physical body and its desires and he'd fallen neatly in the blond man's trap.

There were clear limitations to what such course of action could accomplish now and the dangers he was to encounter were firmly rooted in this world.

In the grip of *gaffla* it was likely that he would make mistakes that would cost them their lives.

"If only I had a good pair of binoculars with me," Brendan said looking up the mountain, "We'd be able to see him then no problem."

The Slinger went to one of the bushes. Using a small blade he cut several long branches, bound them together with twine. From a pocket, he took out a sealed bamboo bottle, smeared a foul smelling black substance on the tips of the branches.

He took out his hood and ripped it into long strips. He then bound them securely to the tip of each branch and smeared the rest of the substance onto them.

"We'll need light," he explained "once inside the mountain," he gave a branch each to Letitia and Brendan and kept one for himself.

"Hey! This is tar!" Brendan said sniffing the substance closely.

The Slinger started climbing.

The mountain face was not very steep, but as darkness fell it became more dangerous.

The deepening shadows lengthened the shape of the outcropping rocks and made it easy to fool the inexperienced eye looking for hand and foot holds.

They climbed for what seemed like hours, endlessly putting one foot after another in a mind-numbing repetitiveness, with only the bright moonlight to guide them.

At one stage the Slinger thought he spied movement, in the darkness ahead and was about to draw their attention to it when the shadow moved again and he realised what it was: a cloud passing across the face of the moon.

Twice Letitia missed her foothold in the dark and slipped down the face and both times she brought herself up short. Fingers clinging desperately onto jugged rocks.

Brendan concentrated on moving carefully ahead. He had put his gun away and secured it and his eyes scouted each rock carefully looking for the best possible hold.

He tested each one before he put his weight on it and moved on.

He was stunned by the Slinger's apparent ability to move over the rocks in the darkness with the speed and agility of a lizard.

They climbed all night, pushed on by the Slinger's relentless energy, always climbing upwards, and daybreak found all three of them, resting aching muscles, grazes and bruises on a ledge, more than halfway up the mountain-face.

"Well done!" the voice came from directly above them.

They crouched for cover and looked up. No more than ten feet above their head, on a protruding ledge, stood the blond man, the tip of a dark cave opening yawned behind him.

Before he had time to think about it the Slinger moved, his hand flicked out twice, lighteningly fast, and two four-pointed stars went spinning through the air.

They bounced harmlessly off the rockface on either side of the blond man's body.

"You don't want to spoil the fun we can have," the blond man smiled, "there must be some questions that'll need answering."

"Eversteen?" Brendan eyed the blond man uncertainly. He looked like Eversteen, the clothes were the same, but the voice, the voice was different.

"Another round eyes? It's getting to be quite a gathering you've got there Rohan.

"However do you manage to attract such throng?"

The Slinger remained silent. Anger and hate danced in his eyes.

"Even a woman to ease the cold nights," the blond man sneered at him derisively, "the rose of Rose, no less. A good choice! How Oda would have approved of it if he were here. Well I'll see you on the other side then? When your burdens shall approximately match mine?"

The blond man disappeared inside the opening and without a word the Slinger moved to follow, the others scrambling to catch up with him.

"He looks like Eversteen," Brendan said to the Slinger as he caught up with his heels, "but what would Eversteen be doing here?"

"The devil has many faces."

They approached the ledge and the Slinger peered experimentally over the side of it, half-expecting some sort of attack. When none came, he pulled himself up onto it and then helped Brendan and Letitia do the same.

The mouth of the cave the blond man had disappeared into was completely dark and lightless. It twisted and turned so that the sun's morning rays, hitting the mountain face from the east, lit only the first few feet, revealing the rock-strewn hollow of a mine shaft.

"In there?" Letitia asked.

"In there," the Slinger said and he struck a sulphur coated stick against his boot and helped them light their torches.

The Slinger turned his back to the rising sun and the light and with the strange man from the sky and the woman who had imposed a blood-bond upon him, following in his wake, he entered the cave of darkness, in the trail of the blond man, the only one who could assuage the craving for revenge that was burning bright inside him.

He had actively chosen this path, whether he knew it or not. All along the way he'd made the crucial decisions that had led him here. Now.

And this, more than anything else, damned him more irrevocably than anything the blond man could do.

Chapter 8

The Mountain Killers

The mineshaft smelled of stale earth and old death.

They were on a narrow path on which the boulders and rocks had been cleared, with rocky walls pressing in on either side of them like rough-hewn cymbals about to crush them.

"I hope it gets wider later on," Brendan said under his breath. He unconsciously clenched and unclenched his right hand, his palm suddenly itched for the reassuring presence of his gun.

"If it doesn't it'll make an ideal place for an ambush," said the Slinger.

Their makeshift torches gave off a flickering light which made the shadows before them tremble and jump and the smoke they gave off stung their eyes and made them stream with tears.

Brendan had his gun out now and was scanning incessantly in front of him, his heart thudding wildly in his chest with the fear of imagined danger, and even Letitia held tightly onto the hilt of the short sword the Slinger had given her as if it could ward off any threat the foul-smelling darkness might throw at them.

They moved in a straight line a few steps from one another, not daring to separate too much.

The mine shaft went down at a steep angle, deep into the bowels of the earth. Above them rose the body of the mountains, a huge, immovable mass through which now the three fragile humans moved.

Whatever thoughts and fears about the future each of them had were now held in abeyance, suspended by the more immediate but invisible threat the mine posed to them.

They walked for what seemed like an eternity, their legs, already tired by the arduous climb up the mountain, moving with a new heaviness that the steep, downward angle of the mineshaft only made worse.

They presently reached some sort of clearing. The rough rock walls that until now had pushed in on them from either side, receded away from them.

"Spoiled for choice or what?" Brendan said.

Several different paths diverged from this spot, each leading into what appeared to be a different direction.

"I take it this was where the motherload of diamonds was," Brendan continued bringing his torch near the rockface.

There were ancient beams soaring up the rock and the roof above their heads, and the chisel marks of man-made digging implements could be clearly seen on the rock.

"Diamonds were mined here," the Slinger confirmed.

Their whispered voices travelled down the shafts rebounding on the rocks to send ghostly echoes back at them. There was nothing to indicate the way the blond man had taken.

"We go down here," the Slinger said, indicating with his torch and setting off first he led them down a steep path that after more than a hundred yards of total darkness broke, without warning, into a cavernous chamber.

The chamber was so large that their torches' light didn't touch the far walls which remained hidden from them. The path they'd followed seemed to cut a straight line through the chamber and at the far end, an opening faintly glowed in the dark.

Outlined with a phosphorescent green light of its own.

"I don't like it here," Letitia said quietly to the Slinger's back.

Judging by the echoes the chamber seemed enormous.

"Wow," was all Brendan could manage. His gun seemed to have been forgotten, hanging limply from his hand by his side.

Ignoring them both, with all his instincts turned on, the Slinger advanced further into the cavern.

Had the blond man come this way?

He was trying to sense the darkness. Read it with his skin as well as his mind. There was something here. Something he could not fathom. Primitive parts of him could barely sense it. Vaguely.

His instincts screamed danger at him.

"Stop," the Slinger commanded hashing Brendan's whisperings.

Instantly there was the whoosh of something thrown through the air and Brendan let out a cry of pain and the .45 spoke.

The bright muzzle-flash of the shot momentarily chased away the darkness and they were all able to see the cavorting spear wielding bodies, the heads noseless with white albino eyes and great shocks of unruly hair, moving towards them from both sides.

"Ainu!" the Slinger yelled drawing his long sword.

Letitia screamed. Brendan, one arm paralysed by a crude spear shaft sticking out of his shoulder, let out an oath and fired again and again. The Slinger became a blur of deadly motion.

He threw his torch into the midst of a group of the fierce creatures and as they backed away from the light, hands raised to shield their sensitive eyes, he was amongst them, his long sword carving up the air in a deadly arc of steel that cleaved arms from bony bodies and heads from scrawny, lizard-skinned necks.

The creatures' foul smelling corpses piled themselves at his feet and still he could feel the pressure of them all around the cavern.

There was a momentary pause in the booming of the .45 as Brendan held the gun between his knees and slapped a fresh magazine in, and Letitia ducked the wild swing

of a rough piece of wood and stabbed the creature, with her sword, in the stomach.

Glassy-eyed, the Ainu staggered back in the darkness that had spawned it and two or three others tripped over the fallen body.

And still they came on.

With a great effort, the Slinger disengaged himself from the mob that surrounded him, leaving piles of bodies trailing behind and reached his two companions.

"We've got to run! To the far end. Can you make it?" he asked Brendan.

After the initial assault the creatures had fallen back, beyond the reach of the light, leaving their dead behind. The Slinger could hear their feet shuffling as they regrouped. The sibilant hiss of their voices filled the darkness with fear.

"I think so," said Brendan. His voice was tight with pain. The Slinger examined the wound in the light of their last remaining torch. The thick leather jacket had stopped most of the force of the blow, but the flint spearhead had still managed to break through to the skin. It was half-embedded between the left edge of Brendan's breast and the tight knot of muscle over his shoulder-joint.

The Slinger grabbed the crude shaft and with a sudden jerking motion pulled the spearhead out. Brendan let out a hoarse cry and his legs buckled, his face suddenly drained of all colour. The Slinger hauled him up roughly by the lapels of his jacket, lifting him like he was a rug doll.

"You've got to stand up," he shouted to his face, "stand up and walk or die right now.

There," he pointed him to the exit glowing faintly in the darkness ahead, "make it to that point over there. After that you'll be free. Free to return to where you came from."

Brendan nodded weakly and clutched his left shoulder tightly. Blood seeped from between his fingers from the wound and dropped to the cave floor lost in darkness at their feet.

"Lead the way chief," he said, but there was no humour left in his voice.

The Slinger turned to Letitia and took hold of her arm. "Are you all right?" he asked and she nodded quickly. Her dark eyes were shining brightly and her face was flushed.

Her chest heaved up and down. "I want you directly behind me," he told her "between me and the stranger, where I can keep an eye on you."

Again she nodded as he explained to her what they had to do.

They started running for the far exit just as the Ainu regained their courage and started to move forward. Twice the Slinger used his sword to slap spears out of the air.

The Ainu, unwisely closed in on them again and the Slinger's sword curved a wide path ahead and to the sides of them before Brendan's booming .45 could drive the creatures back once more.

Brendan kept firing even after the Ainu fell back, each bullet that found its mark lifted its victim off its feet and sent the body crushing into those of its fellows close behind.

Sibilant hissings like the voice of ghosts that had forgotten all human speech rose and fell with each death.

Ainu bodies piled high on the cavern floor. And still they kept shuffling, kept coming at them. The hissing rousing the spectre of superstitious dread in their breasts.

Many times Brendan watched open-mouthed as the Slinger flicked his wrist with superhuman speed to send his silver stars and thin blades into the mass of attacking bodies.

Each time his lethal weapons found their mark.

The Ainu were paying a heavy price for their assault but they were also gaining ground. The Slinger couldn't be everywhere at once and Brendan only had one clip left for his gun.

With a last effort, backs pressed against each other, they made it as far as the exit and the Slinger saw why it was glowing.

The entire, arched structure was made of thick wood, partly rotten in places. The massive frame had bent and buckled, beneath the constant weight of rock it was being asked to shoulder and where the rock face had cracked and broken, droplets of water had run down to soak the wood pores, further weakening the wooden structure.

Fungi had taken root in it. Creatures that lived on the corruption of things. Their white petals gave off the faint glow that had led them to it.

They minute they saw the exit they broke into a run.

"Hurry!" the Slinger said pushing Letitia ahead of him. Brendan came gasping behind.

He turned and fired two more shots into the moving darkness behind him and in the flash of the gun's muzzle the Slinger saw two more creatures fall, but the rest were now almost upon them, the wicked tips of their crude spears waving like the evil claws of death in the darkness.

Pushing Brendan past him, the Slinger took their last torch from Letitia's hands and threw it at the advancing mass of the Ainu. The sudden light made the creatures stop their shuffle and move back, lifting their arms to cover their eyes and the Slinger swung his long sword and brought it hard, down onto the side of the frame of the doorway.

The tempered blade bit deep into the softened wood and rock dust fell all around him.

A spear whistled past him and a thrown rock bounced off the wall to his right but he refused to let this distract him.

He swung his blade again, and again, and each time it bit deeper in the wood, weakening it, and there was the creaking of supports giving way as the roof started to sag. The Slinger then turned and taking hold of his companions, ran, dragging them along with him, as the mountain behind, pressed down upon the ancient beams that had defied it for so long and sent untold tonnes of solid rock to close the opening of the subterranean chamber in which the last few survivors of the fierce Ainu race now lived.

"He's bleeding badly," Letitia said and the Slinger moved to her side to look at Brendan's wounded shoulder.

They were without torches now and had to feel their way in the dark. Faint illumination seeped in from the rocks, further ahead. Brendan was pale and shaking from shock and he was cradling his shoulder.

"I'll be all right," he said through clenched teeth "Let's get out of this place,"

The Slinger picked him up by his good arm and wrapped it round his shoulders. Brendan's breath wheezed with pain.

"Jesus! Be careful!"

"There! Ahead!" the Slinger pointed with his free hand and in the twilight, ahead, they could make out the barely visible dark outline of the blond man running lightly through the dark mineshaft, picking his way through the treacherous passage with preternatural ease.

The darkness made it difficult to calculate the distance separating them. The Slinger thought of the cavern behind them and the entrance he'd just sealed off and the dripping water that had softened the wood and had made the feat possible and he had a brief, nightmarish vision of the rock face above their heads rupturing and waves coming down, crushing them, obliterating them under their sheer weight.

"Stay close to me," he ordered.

Each step was treacherous. The floor of the mine itself had eroded and there were holes revealed underfoot that opened directly into gaping subterranean drops. From time to time their feet dislodged stones and rocks and sent them crushing down and where these pebbles and stones were dislodged they took a long time to echo from the bottom.

"How deep are these mines anyway?" Brendan gasped after the fourth or fifth time this had happened.

"Very deep," said the Slinger.

"Great! PR natural you'd make,"

The Slinger pushed on ahead, testing the treacherous ground and then waiting for them to reach him.

"We are going to get this bastard aren't we?" Brendan kept talking, gaining strength from his own voice. The dull burning in his shoulder now started to turn into a blazing fire and he hoped that whatever the slimy creatures that had fashioned the spear had done, they didn't know about poisons.

"It's getting lighter," Letitia observed and indeed the way ahead was getting lighter, the illumination growing stronger. The fungi that had grown on the rotten wood and outlined the doorway for them, back at the chamber, had found nutrition in the rocks and the piles of earth on either side of the mine shaft floor and now gave off their eerie green light.

The Slinger clumped down on the atavistic fear that rose inside him and refused to speculate on what might have died there in such numbers, to feed the fungi roots.

He turned and went back to where Letitia and Brendan had stopped and stood staring, and taking hold of Brendan's good arm helped the wounded man to his feet.

"Not far to go now," he said, though he didn't even know if they were indeed travelling in the right direction any more.

"As long as you have me back by midnight," Brendan whispered through clenched teeth, "otherwise my mother wouldn't like it,"

They followed the twisting and turning path, changing direction several times, ever going downhill, deeper and deeper into the mountains, until the path started levelling off and presently they came to a point of it where a large section of the entire mineshaft floor had disappeared.

The gap was at least seven feet long and water flowed rapidly underneath. An underground river.

"This is it," Brendan said despairingly, "you've got to leave me here man. No way am I going to make this with one arm,"

The Slinger put down the wounded man and looked at the water and at Letitia and in the faint glow, saw the terror clearly drawn on her face. Alone he could probably jump over the chasm but neither Letitia nor Brendan could be expected to make it.

The Slinger knelt down and looked at the water flowing beneath their feet. There was a clearance between the surface of the water and the mineshaft floor of about a foot.

The water flowed towards the way they were going. The Slinger weighed their chances against all the things that could go wrong. The river could be going deeper underground, or there could be a waterfall, or the roof could slope in, trapping them without air, unable to backtrack because of the strength of the current.

He looked at his two companions and thought that to leave them here would be consigning them to certain death, the mountain was probably riddled with passages and the Ainu, mutants or not would know them all. It wouldn't be long before they appeared again, drawn by whatever promise had made them attack in the first place.

"We've got to go in this," the Slinger said and repeated it in the speech of the People for Letitia and she screamed and shook her head vehemently.

"There's no other way,"

The Slinger took off the long sword from his back and unravelled the scabbard covering to produce a long length of strong twine.

He tied one end of it to Letitia's waist, the other to his own. He then used the rest to fasten Brendan's leather jacket tightly at the sleeves and chest and round the waist.

"It won't hold much air for long," Brendan said seeing what he was doing.

"It's better than nothing,"

The Slinger lowered himself in the water first and held with one hand on the rock, fighting against the full force of the current while they also jumped in.

The water was cold and flowing fast and it gripped them immediately.

The current pulled them under.

The Slinger felt Letitia flail in the water beside him and he pushed off from the bottom, where his boots scraped against loose rocks and debris and he pulled her towards the narrow air pocket overhead.

The flow of the water was rugged and irregular speeding up and slowing down with the opening and narrowing of the tunnel through which it was flowing.

More than once they were bounced against the rough, rocky walls. The Slinger turned on his back and gripping Letitia tightly, pulled her to him.

Her body had gone completely limp and he had to struggle to keep her head above the water.

A little further behind them the bloated, air-buoyed form of Brendan bobbed and bounced on the foamy surface, his face pale like a corpse's.

The underground river walls got progressively narrower, the water itself speeding up, vicious whirls and eddies forming each time the rock sent protrusions into it.

As they were carried helplessly along, the openings of the collapsed mineshaft floor, over their heads became fewer and fewer and it became darker and darker. The feeble illumination of the phosphorescent micro-organisms that fed on corruption, now cut off from them by the solid rock overhead.

The Slinger sensed the increase in the water's speed and kicked out to get further ahead of Brendan's wildly bobbing body. Putting some more distance between them.

His hearing had picked up the noise of water against rock coming from ahead of them and he knew well what it meant. There was a flute somewhere, an opening where the water fell from a height. And they were heading straight for it.

He kept his left arm wrapped round Letitia's neck to keep her afloat and he twisted his body so that he now faced the direction the water was rushing towards.

He risked a quick look over his shoulder but there was nothing to see now but impenetrable darkness, no way to tell if Brendan was still with them. Ignoring the tug of water-blunted rocks on his clothes and chill-numbed flesh, the Slinger turned his body sideways and experimentally sought to reach the tunnel walls.

His boots barely scraped against the rocky walls and at one point his left ankle struck against an underwater protrusion that sent paralysing waves of pain shooting up his leg.

He noticed the tunnel was getting narrower all the time. The water flowing faster.

They rounded a bend and there was now a definite incline in the tunnel floor and there was a little more space to breathe overhead.

The noise the Slinger had first heard was now louder. A dull, threatening throb toward which they almost uncontrollably hurtled.

The Slinger braced himself, timing it perfectly. There was no way he could resist the press of the water at the opening of the flute itself. He knew that, but the first slight bend of the river's course would slow the water down enough to give him the opportunity he needed.

They passed one bend and then another and the water speeded up as the incline of the rock underneath them got steeper and at the third bend, where the water broke into foamy swirls, the Slinger kicked out.

He placed the soles of his boots against the rocky wall to his right and pushed out hard, bracing his shoulders and back against the hard rock behind him and wedging his body, momentarily pitting the strength of his hard, trained muscles against the icy pull of the water and the implacable strength of the current that drove it.

As the Slinger's breath gasped explosively in the darkness and he waited for Brendan's body to cannon into him and dislodge him, the rushing water and his fatigued muscles fought each other.

At first nothing happened. Then, with an almost superhuman effort the Slinger arched his back, pulling his wedged body up and as far above the water's icy clasp as he could manage.

Immediately pain shot through his back, where it was jammed against the rock, the rough face there digging into his flesh. The Slinger ignored it. The years of training took hold and he did what he had to.

His left arm reached out and lifted Letitia above the water, so that only her feet dangled in it now. He then braced himself for the impact as Brendan's body finally cannoned into them and was momentarily caught against Letitia's dangling, limp legs.

For long minutes they remained there, the Slinger supporting them both against the snatch of the current.

"I take it you haven't drowned," Brendan finally coughed and there were spasms of pain colouring his voice.

"The tunnel gets shallower ahead," the Slinger said "there's an opening through which water rushes out. If the drop is not too steep, perhaps we can climb down it."

In the darkness Brendan wondered how he would be able to go down anything. His shoulder was now completely numb, his left arm flopping around, totally useless.

"How's the girl?" he asked, but in the darkness the Slinger gave no answer.

Letitia, held by the Slinger, was a limp weight against them.

Inch by inch, the Slinger crawled along the tunnel, his feet keeping up a constant pressure on the rock, his back getting scraped by the rough surface behind him, the fabric of his tunic being turned into shreds.

Brendan held onto him and the rocky walls, trying in vain to aid him. As he sought to get more purchase in the bottom below his legs were being constantly pulled out from under him by the strength of the flowing water.

Progressing in this painful fashion they finally reached a point where the tunnel walls closed in like a choke and the water rushed past at high speed.

But it was shallow around the sides, the force of it concentrated in the centre. And they found they could resist its push if they held onto the rocky walls for support.

Beyond it the mineshaft above had collapsed to form a natural cave and beyond that the mountain itself had come down so that a huge subterranean cavern had formed.

The water had dug deep in the soft cave floor, etching a furrow through which it flung itself over the precipice and into the expanse of the greater cavern beyond.

It was this noise of water rushing out that the Slinger had first heard.

Apart from the water flowing through the middle of the cave beyond them, the rest of the floor was completely dry. The moisture in the air had worked its miracle accelerating the corruption of organic matter, and everywhere again the luminous fungi had taken root, casting their eerie green glow all over the place.

"Can you stand up?" the Slinger asked.

In the sickly green light Brendan looked like a wakened corpse and Letitia's limp body, her face covered by her long locks of stringy, wet hair, hang like no life would ever inhabit it again.

"I'll try," Brendan coughed.

The three of them, wedged there at the mouth of the flute, looked like flotsam about to be cast into the depthless abyss far below.

Grunting with the agony his hurt shoulder gave him, fighting against the treacherous footing and the pressure of the now knee-high water Brendan managed to gain his feet under him.

"You've got to push past me," the Slinger said, "then I'll pass Letitia's body down to you."

Concentrating on keeping his footing Brendan nodded that he understood.

Twice his good hand slipped from the rock where he'd sought purchase and he was forced to his knees, his wounded shoulder slamming against the rocky wall.

His face ashen, he was at last able to push past the Slinger's straining body and ease Letitia's limp form over the lip of the flute and onto the dry floor of the cave.

The girl he noticed, in the sickly green light, appeared to be breathing. Her small pert breasts, perfectly outlined against the wet fabric of her clothes rose and fell lightly, their dark, high nipples tightly erect from the cold.

She had lost the short sword the Slinger had given her and there was the dark swelling of a bruise on one side of her head where she'd probably been thrown against the rock, but she appeared to be otherwise unhurt.

"I think she's Ok," he said to the Slinger.

The Slinger disengaged himself from his cramped position against the rock and easing himself over the rushing water crouched beside her. The leather of his gloves had been ripped in several places, Brendan saw, and there was now blood from raw palms and knuckles covering his hands.

His long dark hair had been pushed back and his face looked haggard and drawn. His back was a terrible mess.

"A great threat we pose to anybody," Brendan mumbled to himself.

Ignoring his own discomfort the Slinger lifted Letitia's head and examined the bruise on her forehead. He turned her over to her side to empty her stomach and lungs from any water she might have swallowed and waited while she recovered.

Letitia coughed, retched, her body spasmed. Her eyes fluttered open slowly and she saw the Slinger and the stranger looking down at her and she stifled the groan of pain that came to her lips.

"Where are we?" she asked.

The cave they were in was not very long. It had a very wide mouth which opened to a huge subterranean chamber. The luminous fungi were everywhere in large numbers and by their unnatural glow, the Slinger could now see that the size of the chamber their cave opened to was beyond belief.

It stretched high above their heads and its bottom was lost in perpetual darkness. A few feet below the lip of their cave, where the water dropped, was a kind of natural ledge and from there a wooden trellis bridge spanned the black abyss and led across, to the other side where there was a sort of rocky plateau.

"It looks like hell," Brendan whispered behind them.

The inner rock of the mountain rose almost vertically behind the rocky plateau, impossibly smooth from this distance and darkly forbidding.

The water bounced off the ledge beneath the opening of their cave, mere feet from the lip of the bridge and was lost over the side. The bottom of the cavern, where the water struck, was invisible, lost in total darkness. A dull, distant sound came from where it hit bottom.

High up on the far wall, well past the halfway mark between the rocky plateau and the cathedral-like top of the mountain a small opening glowed with natural light.

The way out.

The only way.

It was, the Slinger thought, as if the entire mountain had been hollowed out with only the outer skin left intact. It reminded him of the places of worship which the crazed Shintoists had fashioned in the name of God.

"I think we are near the end," the Slinger said and pointed to the distant opening. "There's daylight coming in from over there,"

"Great. All we need is a good pair of wings," Brendan remarked bitterly.

"Not wings, just strong arms," the Slinger said.

Speaking alternatively to both of them, the Slinger then explained what he proposed they do.

"We'll climb down onto the ledge. One at a time, go over the trellis bridge and then climb up to the opening. That's our way out."

Brendan nodded towards the flimsy contraption of rotted wood and wet rope that was the bridge. "That won't hold us," he said.

"The blond man went that way," the Slinger replied.

"The blond man's a sorcerer," Letitia quietly said, "he said I'll drown beneath waves,"

"The blond man's a traitor," the Slinger said through gritted teeth, "now let's get across."

The first to get down to the ledge was Letitia. The Slinger used the twine that had held her tied to him in the water to lower her as far as he could and then she climbed down the rest of the way on her own.

"Almost there," the Slinger said and Brendan, ashen-faced with pain nodded and smiled weakly and allowed the Slinger to tie the twine around his waist.

"I hope it's stronger than it looks," he joked feebly to the Slinger as the latter took up the slack and positioned himself.

Bracing his legs against the edge of the cavern floor, the Slinger lowered Brendan until his feet could find footholds.

Then with Letitia up on tiptoes, reaching for him to help him balance, Brendan was guided safely onto the ledge and lay with his back pressed against the rock.

He had unzipped his leather jacket now and his chest was heaving mightily beneath it.

The pain made his face seem gaunt, like the skin had been drawn tight against the bones of his skull and there was no blood underneath.

The Slinger slid down unassisted.

The trellis bridge that led to the other side was at least forty feet long and dangerously narrow. There was a heavy rope guide on one side to stop people falling off. The wood of the bridge was stained dark with dump and it glowed with fungi.

The subterranean chamber was so large that all individual sound was lost in it. The water falling beside them seemed to be absorbed by the darkness below in a sort of slow motion display.

"It's like white noise," Brendan mused, "the best way to meditate, they say."

Neither of his two companions listened to what he'd just said. They were both too busy looking at the narrow length of the trellis bridge.

"I'll go across first," the Slinger said to Letitia, "I'll hold the rope for you to follow."

There was nothing to say to this. If he couldn't make it they couldn't either.

The Slinger tested each rung before he put his foot down on it. Had he been physically intact, he would have taken himself half-way up the spirals, reduced his body's weight to that of a feather, floated across the rotten bridge like an avenging angel, eager to get back on the trail of the blond man.

But he was hurt.

Pain assailed him from dozens of cuts and bruises. Ripped and torn muscles and ligaments screamed for his mind's attention. And his back was a flat expanse of white fire. It took all his concentration to ignore the clamouring, clamp down on overexcited nerve-ends and proceed as if nothing had happened.

He couldn't risk the spirals now. It was possible that he would never make it back.

Twice the wood gave way with a sickening, squelching sound beneath his boot. He felt tremors travel all the way along the body of the bridge. He waited until they died out, before he went on.

Step by step he made it across and stepped onto the rocky ledge of the plateau on the other side.

At the last possible instant, with one foot still on the trellis bridge and the other on the solid surface of the rock, he felt the guide rope dissolve and give way beneath his palm and he instantly span around, caught it as it was parting and held the two halves together.

The weight of the rope pulled him forward, stretched his arms to the limit, pulled against his shoulder joints, but he didn't let go.

He remained there, holding the guide rope together. Spreadeagled over the edge of the drop, his feet balancing on the wood at the very edge of the bridge, where the horizontal planks of the rungs of the bridge were joined to the vertical body of the trellis-work.

"Hurry!" he yelled across the span and Letitia hesitated, and then, putting one careful foot in front of the other, began to go across the chasm.

She was about halfway across the bridge when she screamed, lost her footing and staggered. Her hands caught at the guide ropes and the Slinger grunted at the strain of the added weight as the bridge moved.

"I am glad to see you all made it," the blond man said from somewhere above them.

He stood legs spread apart, feet planted firmly on a wide ledge on the rock face directly above their heads.

He was hefting a stone tipped Ainu spear in one hand.

"You bastard!" gasped Brendan from across the way and he pushed himself off the rock behind him. He stood unsteadily at the foot of the trellis bridge and his right hand went inside his jacket, came out tightly griping the .45 and taking aim, trying to steady the shake of his hand

and waving of his body, he fired.

The first shot hit the wall a good foot above the blond man and Brendan cursed. He corrected his aim and fired again.

The bullet this time was much closer though not close enough to be a threat. The sound of the shot boomed briefly in the massive cavern and then there was the dull metal ping of the gun jamming. The ejected cartridge was stuck half-in and half-out of the housing, the spent casing blocking the re-arming mechanism of the gun.

"Poor Lieutenant Brendan. Not very soft posting Clark air base is it?" the blond man sneered and Brendan looked up at him with eyes gone wide.

"Eversteen? It is Eversteen isn't it?"

"Get on the bridge Brendan." the blond man ordered.

"No!" the Slinger said. He could feel the trellis work quiver beneath his feet. Letitia had stopped exactly halfway.

"Get on the bridge," the blond man repeated and hefted the spear aiming it at the Slinger's unprotected, bloodied back and Brendan reluctantly obeyed. He stepped gingerly on the first rung and stood there. Waiting.

"There are so many things we need to talk about. Unfortunately there's never time enough for them all."

"Who are you?" Brendan shouted and the blond man laughed.

"How long do you think the Slinger will be able to hold on? A wager Brendan, what do you say? Longer than it'd take to fly over Mt. Pinatubo?" he suddenly grew serious, "Some know me as the Lamb," he said.

Letitia was shaking. Her eyes were riveted on the blond man and her left hand clutched the bluestone amulet round her neck, her fingers almost white with the pressure she was applying.

The Slinger's body shook. All his energy was concentrated on keeping the two halves of the guide rope from slipping from his hands. The extra weight of Brendan, was making the bridge's structure unstable as the old wood took the added load.

"Would you care to take one more step Brendan?" the blond man motioned with his spear and Brendan hesitated.

Seeing this the blond man changed his aim, pointed the lethal stone tip at the spreadeagled Slinger's back again. "Just beneath the left shoulder blade, I think," he said, "that way I'll be sure to puncture a lung,"

With a grimace of helpless rage Brendan took another step and the blond man, with a laugh, flung his spear at him, hard.

The heavy, stone spearhead struck the centre of the bridge, just beyond the point where Letitia stood and went through the wood like it was water.

The whole structure shook and sagged. Bits of wood broke off and fell soundlessly into the darkness below. Letitia let out a scream as her foot slipped through a hole that appeared and she rolled off the bridge and more boards broke off as her body caught them.

Her hands clutched wildly at the guide rope, caught it at the very last instant, by chance, and as her full weight suddenly pulled on it, it miraculously held and the Slinger was pulled still further forward so that the toes of his boots balanced over the edge, his body held from falling to his death below by the very strain of the guide rope on his shoulders.

His arms felt like they were being pulled off at the joints.

The Slinger held on. Grim visions of death danced in his heart. Letitia vanishing beneath dirty waves. If he couldn't stop this prophecy from coming true he couldn't ever change anything.

Letitia hang in mid-air, the chasm yawned black beneath her feet as she dangled and tried to get her feet to catch on the trellis work so she could get back on the bridge.

On hands and knees Brendan began making his way to her, his face intent on keeping his own balance.

"The bridge will go," the blond man yelled "make your choice Slinger. Go with it, or follow me."

The Slinger held on. The bridge sagged even further and as Brendan's wounded arm gave way beneath him he lost his balance. With a sickening groan the rotten structure collapsed completely, its supports breaking away from the rocky walls to vanish into the nether depths below.

Brendan in turn clung onto the guide rope, hanging on with his good hand. His body swung helplessly over the void.

"Let them go Slinger!" shouted the blond man, "Save yourself, they are dead already."

The Slinger hung grimly on, his entire body shaking violently with the effort. Thick, stinging drops of sweat rolled down his face and into his dark, desperate eyes.

Letitia was limp, she had her eyes shut and tears were streaking down her upturned face. Her breath came in half-choked sobs.

Through the haze of pain radiating from his wounded shoulder, Brendan saw all this. He saw the blond man who looked so much like Eversteen smiling down at him in triumph and the Slinger exhausting every ounce of energy he had left in a desperate attempt to postpone the inevitable and he felt strangely disembodied, his mind detached from the pain and anguish his senses read.

There was, he felt, the intimation of an invisible dimension pervading the scene. A sense of a cosmic struggle to which he and Letitia were only inadvertent participants who had accidentally stumbled into the fray. Doomed from the very beginning.

"Let go!" he shouted and the Slinger arched his back the chords of his neck standing out with the effort, and grimly held on. "Damn it let go! You can't save us! There are more worlds than the one you know!"

His words hang in the air like a prophecy.

The meaning of them startled Brendan himself. He dispassionately wondered where it had come from. Where? Why?

With an anguished cry the Slinger felt his sorely tried muscles betray him, the rope slipped through his left hand, burnt a furrow, through the tattered glove, and opened the flesh beneath it to the bone. His body, clinging to the shorter length of rope with his right hand, was swung hard against the rock, bruising his already badly damaged back.

Letitia fell with an agonised wail. Her body spun in space beside Brendan's their outstretched hands almost touching.

As they were both swallowed by the darkness below, the Slinger thought he heard a deep splash and he had a heart-rending vision of waves closing over Letitia's head, the murky water rushing down her throat, filling her lungs, and he threw his head back and ineffectually howled his anguish.

Pooling the last of his strength, hand over hand, he hauled himself up to the ledge and lay on the hard rock of the plateau, breathing heavily. There was no part of his body that didn't hurt. He lifted his head but the blond man was nowhere to be seen, the ledge on the rockface, on which he'd stood, was now empty.

The Slinger pulled his long sword from its shoulder scabbard and grasped the cold steel between his teeth and with a desperate strength born of inhuman fury he attacked the rockface and began to climb up the wall, towards the opening, through which fresh air and light poured.

He clawed his hands in the rock, looking for handholds, his breath came in agonised gasps and wherever his split-open left hand touched, it left a trail of red, glistening behind, to mark his passage.

His climb seemed removed from all time-scales so that every inch that he gained took lifetimes of labour and his mind, blanked by pain and agony and guilt and remorse felt the fabric of reality crinkle and the blond man's enchantment took hold, at last, and the wall to which the Slinger clung on, began to pulsate with unnatural energy.

The Slinger felt his hold on his senses sway and with his last tattered remnants of strength, he focused his consciousness and his mind, trained and versed in the existence of the invisible that extended the Way of the Sword and made human miracles possible, finally called upon *Kobudera* and the shadows of his ancestors, and as the spirals began their inexorable pull, he judged the moment finely, waited until his strength faded from his limbs and at last allowed his grip on the present to relax.

And he fell.

There was no cry as his body cut through the air and there was no sound but silence, and the very rock seemed to blur, its pulsating life obscenely following his fall, and at the touch of the Slinger's torn body, it responded and opened up, inviting, welcoming, warm as a womb, and accepted his form.

The Slinger was gone.

In his place was left a luminous presence.

He felt his body as a distant thing, a minor manifestation of a greater consciousness of which his entire existence was only a speck and all that had happened to it were but mere annoyances, events that pointed to new, unexplored directions, small steps that had to be taken in order to arrive at the Truth, the ultimate force that ruled the Universe.

The truth was that in this Universe he was dead.

It was a death unlike any other because it enabled him to shed off his humanly imposed constraints and unleash his sight to encompass every dimension. His memories became echoes upon a manifold path on which he was merely a shadow.

Yame, aptly named.

With his new sight he looked back, saw Brendan bathed in uncertainty, a victim caught between two worlds, wreathed in smoke from an explosion which no human agency could control.

He saw Letitia, a finely tuned instrument of sensual delight, afflicted by the entire need of mankind. He saw her role in the course of Time and she had the ability to succour and comfort and her power, quenched forever beneath the dirt laden waters, burnt bright.

He saw his past, and his future, and more.

And there was pain.

But it was not physical pain, of course. It spiked his soul which his body encapsulated and told him of failings and the things he could have averted but hadn't. The treachery he should have avoided and didn't. And as he looked deep inside himself there were thoughts of Yukio and what she'd suffered and Rei, sweet Rei and the Slinger's soul could take no more and all the definitions of himself he had so carefully fashioned in a world of beauty and light and love, finally snapped and were dissolved.

He began then to redraw that seamless energy that was his being and he knew partly, where he was. He listened then to the voices coming through the rock for direction and with a thought stopped his fall through the warm body of rock that had somehow nurtured him, and sought the whereabouts of his physical self.

He realised that throughout his fall he'd been climbing, and as his physical body continued its ascend up the rock, he felt the receding dance of the spirals and began to descend, towards the place where he would join it and the price of *gaffla* that he knew would have to be paid.

When the Slinger finally climbed out of the cavern, three days had gone by, his wounds had healed and his rage was no more. His face shone with the inner glow of the newly-born and there was a ponderousness about his movements, a maturing of presence that marked the beginning of the evolution of slow thought processes, reaching some yet invisible peak.

The blond man was sitting cross-legged in the shade of a broad-leaf frond and he smiled as soon as he saw him.

"Come with me," he said and stood up and motioned for the Slinger to follow him.

"I'm going to kill you," the Slinger said quietly and the blond man didn't lose his smile.

"In time, perhaps," he said "Come with me," and he led, and the Slinger followed.

Chapter 9

The Awakening

The blond man took the Slinger to a place where the grass flowered and the plains were dressed in colours of green and yellow and red and the sun radiated that special warmth that makes the earth come alive.

"This is your Eden," the blond man said and the Slinger, who'd never heard of the word looked blankly at him and said nothing.

Wherever the Slinger looked he saw life awakening, renewed, as if from a long slumber and only he remained untouched by the joy he was witnessing. There was a hollowness deep inside him, where his purpose had once burnt bright.

The Slinger concentrated on the straight flow of the blond man's back and he tried, with all his senses, to feel some of the blond man's black power. But the surrounding life radiated so strongly that whatever the blond man had inside him, was completely masked so that every time the Slinger shut his eyes, the blond man registered as an emptiness.

A void in human form.

Like new centurions, afresh from a crucifixion, the two figures trudged up a hill, the blond man leading in front, the Slinger following a step behind and at the top they stopped by a pile of stones and wordlessly sat and looked at each other.

The blond man put down the pack he'd been carrying with him and from it he took out a tin pot and two fine bone china cups and a bottle of water and a small leather bag of finely ground tea-leaves. The bag had been greased on the outside to water-proof the leather and its mouth closed with air-tight clasps the likes of which the Slinger had never seen before.

"Tea?" the blond man motioned with the cups and the Slinger gave him an expressionless shrug.

The blond man spent a long time, carefully measuring the water in the cups, pouring it into the tin pot, putting the tea inside and finally, when the ritual was complete, he held the tin pot aloft in his left hand and with his right he made an intricate sign in the air and there was a red glow, all around the base of the tin pot, and the water boiled.

The Slinger watched all this in his own wordless fashion, his eyes gauging the power the blond man displayed, his fingers toying with the hilt of his sword. The blond man filled a cup with tea and ritually offered it to him and the Slinger, his mind suddenly awash with the memory of the untouched, untasted tea that Yukio had offered him in the past, unsheathed his long sword with the hiss of cold steel and stuck it in the soft ground, beside him. His right hand then reached out and accepted the cup.

And so it came to pass that in a place of beauty, the Slinger sat opposite his adversary and listened to the blond man's words.

"It is time you understood a few things," the blond man said and this time his voice was soft and quiet and there was a note of melancholy colouring it.

"This is the crossroads, the cusp of many worlds. There are many beginnings here, as many as there are men in the world. And for every man and every man's dreams there are that many worlds, all passing through this very place.

"There are certain laws keeping the structure together. Men have long tried to understand them, to encompass them in their myths, to encapsulate them in the workings of their science. Some have come close, very close indeed, others have failed from the beginning. Some of those who've failed have managed to find the antipodes, the dark side of the realm, others still have completely ignored them, neglected the truth of their nature as they sought out the light, and they have gone mad."

"Why are you telling me all this?" the Slinger asked.

"Because there's a need for you to know. We now are equal, you and I. You carry the burden of the girl's soul, the unpaid debt of her saving you. Nothing happens without a reason. I know something about debts, and burdens, believe me. It's not very pleasant, which is why you must understand."

"Who are you?"

"I am not Eversteen," the blond man laughed, "though I suppose I could have been, in another life, probably was, flying has always fascinated me you know. The freedom of space, the dying- At least it's always different."

The blond man stopped talking and took a swill from his cup and smacked his lips in appreciation. "A good cup of tea," he said, "good for the soul, little pleasures like that. Why there's even an entire empire that built its strength on the sale of tea. Can you imagine that?"

The Slinger took a tentative sip from his cup. The tea was strong, aromatic, but nothing more. Without taking his eyes off the blond man for an instant, he drunk.

"Of course it's not easy," the blond man said, "this business of accepting a burden. But when the order of the worlds is at stake I'm afraid drastic measures are required. Flawed souls. It is an axiom I suppose, only from flawed tools may perfect works be wrought and you, and - I, are flawed, you can be certain of that."

"You must have a name." said the Slinger.

"Yes, I suppose I did, once. When your father presented me to the emperor. I was called...Paul."

"Paul? But you were the-"

"The Seer?" the blond man laughed, "Yes, well, that was later, much later, after the reshuffle of the worlds. Your father was a great believer in magic, he thought it would solve it all."

"And you killed him."

The blond man looked pained. "I was responsible for his death, yes. But by then his friend, Paul, was gone. Only I remained, changed, even as you will be, Slinger."

The blond man's voice droned on talking of the strange concept of worlds within worlds. How Time and Space exist within the Mind and that Mind is large and luminous and it sends off little sparks.

The human mind always aspired to commune with the Mind but it could not understand anything about its nature any more than creatures so small that a man could squash them underfoot without even noticing, could hope to understand what drives the world of man.

The Slinger had no ground from which to intuit the meaning of many of the things the blond man said, and understand, so he sipped his aromatic tea and brooded darkly and listened to the words of his adversary, and searched inside himself for the strength to carry out his revenge.

"You destroyed my world," the Slinger said.

"All things must come to an end," said the blond man, "Even the Slingers. Have you learnt nothing in your travels? Lives that manage to burn so brightly attract more than their share of trouble," he took another long sip from his cup of tea.

"And you, you Slingers, you managed to burn so bright. Setting yourselves almost impossible tasks. The incorruptible defence of the Law. Didn't you know of things such as this is the Balance upset?"

"The Balance?"

"Your father set off so many things by coming here Rohan. I am little more than a conduit, a catalyst. Men see in me that which they fear the most. Your father never understood that."

"There were so many innocent-"

"Innocence, Rohan, is a matter of perspective. The blood of the innocent is what buys back the Balance, resets the laws that govern the worlds. It has always been that way, people must suffer if they're to be reborn."

"You betrayed us," the Slinger's voice was dangerous.

"You betrayed yourselves! Slingers followed me!"

"No!"

"Musashi realised the truth."

The Slinger's fingers tightened around the grip of his sword but this was the crossroads, as the blond man had said, the ground where he was most powerful. The blond man snapped his fingers and everything was transported into darkness.

If the Slinger had found the darkness beneath the mountains bad, this was a thousand times worse. The darkness now, was palpable. Against all reason, it had mass, a living, tactile body that invaded all pores, entered through every opening, became a lightless medium through which the Slinger existed, so that he was an indivisible part of it and his body added to the weight of the darkness oppressing him.

"I have failed," the Slinger said to himself, "I have failed," and through his mind flashed Musashi's words and he took stock of his fear and marshalled his energy and felt the weight inside him ease a tiny bit.

He moved a little then, though it was so dark he couldn't see his limbs and suddenly he could think again.

"Very good, you are learning," the disembodied voice of the blond man said from somewhere around him and the Slinger struggled to see him. His stretched his arms out in front of him, fingers hooked into murderous claws, but there was nothing to feel.

They both swam, quite naturally, in pure void.

Some time later, as he hang in the darkness, listening to the sound of his own heartbeat, he had a vision of many worlds, each removed from the next by an infinitesimal particle, so small and so fast that it vibrated in and out of sixteen dimensions at once.

There were worlds where the People had failed, their race gone forever, and others where the round eyes and the People lived side by side and others still populated by strange, deformed, shadowy creatures that bore no resemblance to anything human and on and on, it went, so that in all this infinity there was every conceivable form and every conceivable life. And it was all happening at the same time.

The Slinger found that he could focus, pick out details from many worlds, and his sight showed him individuals.

Here was Letitia and she'd never been publicly flogged. There was

Musashi, bent and old passing his post to Oda, here was a man he didn't know drinking water from a poisoned well, there was his father dabbling in arcane spells.

He felt more than saw the imbalance. He didn't know what caused it but the worlds now changed, many of them went dead, new, grotesque possibilities came to life and as his father leaped from one to the other, a tiny spark. The Slinger felt an ethereal presence imperceptibly move, completely unseen: a threat, and he yelled: "No!"

The worlds vanished.

"Now you begin to understand," the disembodied blond man said, the Slinger could

still not see him.

"Let me out!" the Slinger yelled.

"Not before you experience the end," said the blond man's voice.

The Slinger felt a shift in the body of the darkness, like a rogue cell, he felt himself transported to every tiny pore of it and inside himself he felt that the darkness was really a light. A light so bright that it burnt the retina of his eyes and forever put out his sight.

He felt the dark heat of this light and drew himself into a protective ball and the light absorbed him, welcomed him, enfolded him and for the last time in his life the Slinger experienced love.

Though it seemed to last forever, it was only an instant long.

The blond man brought them slowly out of the darkness, back on the hill. The landscape was different now, the green grass was studded with row upon row of orderly crosses. They were fashioned of brilliant white marble and their long stems and cross-arms picked up and reflected the light from the sun.

"Let's walk," the blond man suggested and side by side they strolled down the hill, into the graveyard.

There were names of all nations chiselled on the crosses the Slinger saw. "What is this?" he asked.

The blond man didn't answer.

They presently came upon a natural corridor in the rows of crosses and as they turned the Slinger saw the words upon a grave, the marble cross, radiant:

LT. JOSEPH P. BRENDAN

U.S.A.F. CLARK AIR BASE
PHILIPPINES, 1964-2007.

The Slinger stared at the hard-chiselled characters silently for a long time. Had the man from the sky ever lived? He thought, did he really die in the bowels of the earth?

There were many things he didn't understand.

Seeking some familiar ground to stand upon, he sought to rekindle his hate for the blond man and recited his personal mantra to himself but the words rang hollow in him this time, without conviction. He had been into the light and knew that he had no strength for this death.

"When I looked unto those worlds," said the Slinger "I never saw you, or myself."

The blond man hummed, looked around as if taking a last look at a place he was going to leave. Dark clouds broiled overhead and covered the sky. The blond man looked up.

"It is almost time," he said sadly.

They turned and walked back up the hill, where the Slinger's long sword, stuck in the earth, waited patiently, marking the site for their return.

"You couldn't see yourself, or me," the blond man said, "We simply do not exist. We are the Mind's answer to imbalances. The sacrificial lambs.

"Every time this happens a Champion is chosen. This time it has to be you, I have done my part."

The Slinger thought of the words of the oracle he'd been given after he came out of the desert. There had been three days before the blond man's trap had tied him to Letitia and three days spent in the rock, after her death. He thought he could see how things fell into place and felt a strong sense of detachment as he surveyed inside him all that had happened, his mind was slow to understand, slow to grasp.

The blond man read his thoughts. "It is no good to seek to bury your guilt in the words of the oracle. The I Ching, reads a different score to the present."

"Must there be hurt then?"

"Yes."

"I'll find another way."

"There's no other way. Let's go."

And so they returned to the hill they started from and the blond man and the Slinger stood facing each other, separated by the sword and the blond man wrapped his fingers around the hilt and pulled the blade from the ground and there was a last flicker on the metal from a ray of the sun, before the sky was completely covered by cloud.

"I am not ready for this," The Slinger said, "I don't even know what it is I am supposed to do."

"Oh, you will, my friend, you will. After all," the blond man's familiar smile lifted the corners of his mouth once more, "How can you fail to become the very thing you so intensely hunt?"

"Let us then speak the truth."

"Yes, let us."

"Why did you betray us?"

The blond man's eyes sparkled hard, like emeralds but the smile on his lips was sad.

"I am not in control of people's destinies Rohan, I am just a conduit. The catalyst that creates the Champions, the cause of the quest that strips them of their mortal self.

"Remember I told you in the Keep, circumstances choose who the people will follow."

"You also spoke about a star and later with Yukio-"

"People make their own choices Rohan. You'll come to appreciate this in time. I took nothing that was not freely offered."

"And the curse?"

"You easily disproved that."

"You controlled me from the very beginning, then."

"No, I just guided you to seek your soul. It is necessary that you understand your true nature before you attempt to restore the Balance. Did the rock and the spirals teach you nothing?"

"Was that your work then too?"

"Yes, mine and more."

The blond man's words were rife with mystery. And he offered the Slinger back his sword.

"I don't have to do this." the Slinger said.

"No, you don't. This is your choice. We made many mistakes, your father and I, Rohan. Let it be, back to the origins then my friend, back to the sky." he looked up at the heavy sky above, "I don't envy you."

The Slinger's eyes locked into the blond man's gaze and a secret form of understanding passed between them, it had to be this way. Acting with a will that was born out of necessity, the Slinger took the sword from him and ran the blond man through, expiating by this very act, the guilt of his crimes, wiping the slate clean for the both of them.

The blond man dropped to his knees, "Thank you," he whispered once and fell flat on his face, dead.

It was an empty act of revenge, as much his own as the blond man's and the Slinger knew this. It had accomplished nothing but given one man release. Of such small things is the Balance formed. The Slinger felt the burden of this knowledge: the fact that his work had began with a death.

He recalled the words Rei had said to him when he'd first kissed her sweet lips: "The burden of our actions may extend beyond our strength to survive them, my love."

A wind picked up and ruffled the hair of the blond man, lying at his feet, his blood stilled, and the Slinger heard the ghostly voices of old friends saying goodbye.

With heavy heart he left the hill that was the crossroads, the place of peace where death was performed. And he looked back only once, at the endless rows of crosses, a reminder that there does all life end: upon the killing ground.

As he walked, deep inside him, the Slinger felt the layers of awareness unpeeling, a coming of age that had nothing to do with tests of manhood, and the scales fashioned long ago, when he had been happy, fell from his eyes and he finally witnessed the truth of what he had become.

The blond man had been right, he had changed. Once he had been human. Now, he wasn't so sure.

His legs took him away from the green plains behind him, and the rows of marble crosses and the terrain changed once more. It was now dark and desolate, bereft of the colours of flowers and the green of the grass, but the Slinger was beyond noticing any of this.

His mind was deep in the awakening of intense awareness, deep in the pain of passing. He relived parts of the life he'd forgotten, and realised the scope he had, the opportunity, to make all the wrong choices.

This, he couldn't understand. How could the Mind accept such threat to its creations?

A cold wind blew around him. The Slinger remembered a land ruled by men like him, with the dragon star on their chest. The Law was served then. Successive generations saw to it.

He was the first. Now he was alone. The last of his kind left in the world, possibly in all of creation.

He looked up and saw that as he'd walked the world had changed yet again.

He came to the shore of a lake and in his right hand he still clutched the bloodied sword. He carefully wiped the blade and sheathed the weapon in its scabbard on his back.

The wind had fallen and the surface of the lake was still, mirroring the heaviness of the brooding sky above. The lake stretched as far as the eye could see without sign of land. A watery world, drowning every feature which the eye could have used to rest upon.

He sat there, and breathed deeply and felt the calmness of Zen approaching him. The No-mind he had coveted fro so long. And he realised how long he had been without calmness and he allowed it to fill his hollow being, to weigh his body down, firmly fixing his presence in the world: a sole human being at the empty shore of an endless lake.

His thoughts went to the world he had known, which was no more, and he realised just how much Zen had guided all life then.

Now, he thought, it too will eventually be lost.

Darkness was coming, disruption, and he would have a task to perform. He could fail in this, he had his own pain, his own burdens of the soul and although the blond man had said they would make him strong, the Slinger had reason to doubt.

He thought, perhaps there is no reason why I should be expected to save the world.

He'd lived through enough pain already.

As he sat there, waiting, many thoughts fleetingly crossed his mind. He thought that he didn't feel ready for this, the struggle that was lying ahead, but then, he supposed, there could be no adequate preparation for war against a nameless threat. An enemy whose nature was unclear even to those who prepared to fight him.

A storm was brewing above his head, dark clouds rolled threateningly along the horizon.

The Slinger sat utterly still. Tears flowed down his cheeks.

As the sun went down, behind the clouds covering the sky, he felt the deep loss of happiness and, truly alone now, he mourned.

THE END

www.fantasynovel.co.uk

The adventure goes on...

Japanese character for Spring - season of hope